Becky caught her breath as she got her first glimpse of the world-famous star. Isabella was very slender and slight, and was somewhat shorter in real life than she looked on-screen. But she was just as beautiful, with her very long, very dark hair and her tanned, golden skin.

Isabella smiled warmly as she posed on the steps for pictures. There were more cheers from the fans, who were now waving their autograph books, trying to attract Isabella's attention, while the photographers' flashguns blazed away as they shot picture after picture of the star. As Lauren's dad hurried forward to welcome the actress, Becky gave herself a mental shake. This was it! Time to put their plan into action . . .

Also available in

The
**Mayfair
Mysteries**
series:

THE CASE
of the Poisoned Pie

The Mayfair Mysteries

THE CASE
of the Ruby Necklace

Alex Carter

RED FOX

THE MAYFAIR MYSTERIES: THE CASE OF THE RUBY NECKLACE
A RED FOX BOOK 978 1 849 41171 4

Published in Great Britain by Red Fox Books,
an imprint of Random House Children's Publishers UK
A Random House Company

This edition published 2011

3 5 7 9 10 8 6 4

Series created and developed by Amber Caravéo
Copyright © Random House Children's Books, 2011
Cover illustration by Katie Woods

Set in Stempelschriedler

Red Fox Books are published by Random House Children's Publishers UK,
61–63 Uxbridge Road, London W5 5SA

www.**randomhousechildrens**.co.uk
www.randomhouse.co.uk

Addresses for companies within The Random House Group Limited can be found at:
www.randomhouse.co.uk/offices.htm

THE RANDOM HOUSE GROUP Limited Reg. No. 954009

A CIP catalogue record for this book is available from the British Library.

The Random House Group Limited supports The Forest Stewardship
Council (FSC®), the leading international forest certification organisation.
Our books carrying the FSC label are printed on FSC® certified paper.
FSC is the only forest certification scheme endorsed by the leading
environmental organisations, including Greenpeace. Our
paper procurement policy can be found at
www.randomhouse.co.uk/environment

MIX
Paper from
responsible sources
FSC® C016897

Printed and bound in Great Britain by Clays Ltd, St Ives PLC

With special thanks
to Narinder Dhami

Lauren

Eye colour: blue

Hair: auburn – like the rest of the family – cut into a bob

Style: jeans, T-shirts and Converse

Siblings: Charlie, an annoying little brother

Likes: anything sporty, especially swimming in the lush hotel pool

Dislikes: tidying her room

Prize possession: mobile phone, for keeping the other girls up to date with all the action at the Mayfair Park

Dreams of: running her own chain of luxury hotels, one in LA, New York, Paris, Dubai . . . a home on every continent!

Jas

Eye colour: brown

Hair: shoulder length Afro-Caribbean curls

Style: glam and wild! Favourite items include super-sparkly shoes and anything with animal print

Likes: spending time with her BFFs

Dislikes: sitting still, Maths lessons, sitting still in Maths lessons . . .

Secret talent: impressive acting skills – useful in getting the girls out of several sticky situations with The Snoop

Dreams of: becoming the next Beyoncé or Tyra Banks – Jas is definitely the diva of the group!

Mia

Eye colour: brown

Hair: very long, very dark, shiny and straight

Style: eclectic – Mia mostly wears bright colours, layered with one of her mum's vintage Spanish scarves

Siblings: two geeky older brothers

Likes: all animals, especially those in need of some TLC

Prize possession: a top-of-the-range laptop – Google can help solve almost any mystery!

Dreams of: working for the United Nations, or becoming a vet

Becky

Eye colour: grey

Hair: blonde, shoulder-length curls

Style: pretty and girly . . . floaty skirts, floral tops and high heels

Likes: organizing things for everyone, especially her forgetful dad . . . and chocolate!

Dislikes: untidiness – the total opposite of super-messy Lauren!

Prize possession: her collection of celeb memorabilia. The Mayfair Park is the perfect place for celeb-spying . . .

Dreams of: being a high-flying celebrity agent – Becky was born super-glam and super-organized!

CHAPTER ONE

Hurry up and get round here as fast as u can – got a gr8 big surprise for u all!!! Lauren x

Her blue eyes dancing with mischief, Lauren Bond hit the SEND button on her phone and forwarded the mysterious text to her best friends, Mia, Becky and Jas. Her mates would be *dying* to find out what was going on, Lauren thought gleefully. She'd hardly been able to believe it herself when her parents had told her earlier that morning. Now she couldn't wait to see the looks on her friends' faces when she told them the amazing news . . .

I bet Jas is first to get here! Lauren thought, smiling to herself. Her phone beeped, signalling that she had a text, and she flipped it open and read the message.

Ooh, can't stand the excitement! Tell me!!! Jas x

Typical Jas – she was always in a rush and could never wait for anything!

No way! Not until you get here! Lauren texted back, adding a kiss and a smiley face.

Lauren curled up more comfortably in a corner of the squashy black leather sofa and glanced around the huge hotel reception, its interior tastefully decorated in cream and blue. It was Saturday morning and the hotel was busy with weekend guests. Some were checking in, others were checking out, and the smart glass-and-chrome café-bar on the far side of reception was full of people enjoying breakfast. Although it was still quite early, the hotel spa, swimming pool and gym were already busy. Lauren had been for an early-morning swim, and the spa had already been filling up with guests relaxing in white robes.

Lauren sighed with contentment. She'd been absolutely thrilled when her parents had come to work at the Mayfair Park, a luxury hotel in London. Her dad was the hotel manager and her mum was head of hospitality, and although most of the staff lived off the premises, Lauren, her younger brother Charlie and their parents had a flat in a wing of the hotel.

Lauren *adored* living at the Mayfair Park. She never got bored with people-watching because there was always so much going on. Lauren loved everything, from the huge, noisy kitchens where Louis Henri, the temperamental French chef, ruled with a rod of iron and produced mouth-wateringly delicious meals for the hotel restaurant, right up to the exclusive luxury suites on the top floor. She just couldn't imagine living anywhere else. Mia, Becky and Jas loved hanging out at the hotel too, so whenever the girls got together out of school, it was always at the Mayfair Park. Lauren's parents were very laid-back about the girls being in the hotel and using the facilities, as long as they didn't annoy any of the guests or get in their way.

At that moment Lauren's dad popped out of his office near the reception desk to shake hands with a group of departing American guests.

'What a fabulous hotel you have, Mr Bond,' one of the women in the party said in a Southern drawl. 'We've enjoyed our stay so much.'

'It's been a pleasure,' Lauren's dad replied. 'We look forward to seeing you again in future.' As the guests left, he waved at Lauren and then disappeared back into his office.

A few minutes later Lauren spotted her mum on the other side of reception. Mrs Bond looked brisk and efficient in her dove-grey trouser suit with her wavy auburn hair, the exact same shade as Lauren's short bob, tied neatly back. Clipboard in hand, she was deep in discussion with a couple of her assistants. There was a big medical conference taking place at the hotel over the weekend, and Lauren's mum was in charge of organizing it.

Lauren felt a rush of enormous pride. It was her parents who between them kept the hotel running smoothly and efficiently, and they were *brilliant* at it . . .

Suddenly Lauren sat up as Jas, long legs flying, came dashing up the marble steps between the stone columns that flanked the entrance to the hotel. Lauren giggled quietly to herself. Jas never walked anywhere if she could run. She watched Jas say a breathless hello to the doorman, James, looking very smart in his blue and gold uniform, and then hurry into reception, weaving her way between guests and their suitcases.

Lauren waved. Jas's face lit up when she spotted her and she rushed straight over.

'Hi, Lols,' she said, plonking herself down on the sofa next to Lauren. 'So, come on, spill it! What's going on?'

Lauren shook her head tantalizingly. 'I couldn't *possibly* say until Mia and Becky get here,' she replied.

'*Nooooo!*' Jas groaned, ruffling her shoulder-length black hair in frustration. She dived into her jeans pocket and pulled out a bar of chocolate. 'Not even for *this*?'

'Bribery and blackmail won't get you anywhere,' Lauren said firmly, her eyes twinkling.

'Then I'll just have to eat it myself,' Jas sighed, unwrapping the chocolate. But, with a grin, she broke it in two and gave half to Lauren.

'It must be something to do with the hotel,' Jas speculated knowingly as they ate the chocolate. 'Can't you just give me a teeny-tiny little clue?'

'No,' Lauren retorted. 'No, no, NO! No clues!'

'I guess that's a no, then,' Jas said with a pretending-to-be-offended sniff.

'You won't have to wait much longer,' Lauren went on. 'Here's Mia now.'

Mia was coming up the steps. She smiled shyly at James and then slipped quietly through the glass doors, stopping to pick up a newspaper and hand it back to the guest who'd dropped it.

'I *thought* you'd be here first, Jas,' Mia remarked with a smile as she joined Lauren and Jas on the sofa. 'Have you been attempting to bribe Lauren with chocolate?'

'Ooh, as if I'd do such a thing,' Jas said with mock-indignation, breaking off some of her own chocolate and handing it to Mia. 'What a totally suspicious mind you have, Mia Lopez.'

'She tried, but I didn't give in,' Lauren added, winking at Mia.

'That figures!' Mia laughed, flicking back her long shiny waterfall of dark hair. Mia was so pretty, with her gorgeous hair and big brown eyes, Lauren thought, as she'd done a million times before. But Mia was so quiet and un-assuming, she didn't even seem to realize. 'Look, Becky's just arrived.'

Becky was strolling confidently up the steps, blonde curls bouncing. She smiled at James and walked into reception, looking around until she spotted the other girls waving madly at her.

'Sorry I'm late, guys. My dad decided to cook bacon and eggs this morning, and managed to set his tie on fire!' Becky rolled her eyes. 'Honestly, how can a Professor of Environmental Bio-geochemistry be *so* useless in the kitchen?'

'I don't even know what Biogeochemistry is,' Mia said.

'Neither do I!' Becky confessed as Lauren handed her some chocolate.

'Oh, never mind about bio-whatcha-ma-call-it!'

Jas said impatiently. 'Now we're all here, can you *please* tell us what's going on, Lols?'

'She doesn't need to,' Becky butted in, amusement in her wide-set grey eyes. 'I've already guessed!'

Lauren stared at her, amazed. 'You can't *possibly* know, Becks,' she declared. 'It only happened this morning.'

'Tell us, Becky,' Jas demanded eagerly.

Becky shrugged. 'Well, I reckon Lauren has *finally* tidied up her bedroom and she's invited us all round here to admire it!'

Lauren burst out laughing. Whenever Becky came to the Mayfair Park, she was always desperate to get her hands on the (admittedly terrible) mess in Lauren's bedroom and tidy it all up. Becky was the queen of organization and efficiency. Secretly Lauren really admired her friend because ever since Becky's mum had died a few years ago, she'd been left on her own with her absent-minded-professor dad. Somehow Becky was managing to cope very well.

'If that's all it is, I'm afraid I shall have to get *extremely* angry, and shout and throw things,' Jas said sternly. She threw Lauren a beseeching glance. 'It's *not* that, is it, Lols? *Please* tell me it isn't.'

'As if!' Lauren laughed.

'OK, then, I think I know what it is.' Mia flashed Lauren a cheeky grin. 'Lauren has finally gone all girlie and bought herself a dress! Or maybe some lip-gloss?'

Lauren looked horrified, and this time it was Jas, Mia and Becky's turn to burst out laughing.

'No way!' Lauren exclaimed. She wasn't into stuff like clothes and make-up at *all*. 'Come on, let's go up to our flat, and I'll tell you there. Charlie's gone for a swim with his mate Joe, so at least we won't have him hanging around, annoying us.'

'OK, but I think we'd better hurry,' Becky said, 'otherwise Jas is literally going to burst with excitement, and that could get very messy!'

The girls jumped to their feet and headed across reception, Lauren leading the way. There were six lifts close by, and the girls summoned one to take them up to the first floor, where Lauren's flat was.

'Mia, I hate to worry you, but your bag appears to have a life of its own,' Becky remarked as they stood in the lift. Lauren and Jas both stared down at Mia's embroidered Indian bag and saw that a corner of it was bulging and twitching.

'It's Dillon,' Mia explained as they piled into the lift. 'He's a bit off-colour, so I'm keeping an eye on him.'

'And who is Dillon?' Jas enquired as the lift zoomed upwards.

'One of my gerbils,' Mia replied solemnly. She opened her bag and Lauren, Becky and Jas peeped in. A tiny, furry gerbil was settling down in the corner, next to a handful of seeds.

'Hi, Dillon,' Lauren said, stroking the gerbil gently with her finger. Mia loved animals and had a whole menagerie of pets – gerbils, rabbits, cats, dogs and guinea-pigs – at the home she shared with her parents and two older brothers.

'Can Dillon breathe OK inside that bag?' Becky asked.

'Course he can!' Mia replied a little indignantly. 'Dillon really enjoys coming everywhere with me!'

'Remind me never to visit London Zoo with Mia,' Jas said as Mia closed her bag again. 'Who knows *what* kind of animal she might try to smuggle out? Enormous, hairy-scary tarantula, anyone?'

The girls laughed as the lift drew to a halt and the doors slid open. Lauren's heart sank, though, as she saw the tall, thin, upright figure of Mrs Stoop, the hotel's housekeeper, standing outside.

'Good morning, girls,' was all Mrs Stoop said as she stepped into the lift. But she didn't smile, and Lauren could see that she looked distinctly annoyed. Mrs Stoop – or The Snoop as the girls called her – was excellent at her job, but she'd never approved of Lauren, Charlie and their friends hanging out at the hotel. She had often complained to Lauren's dad about it.

'I know The Snoop is just *dying* to catch us doing something naughty so she can tell my parents,' Lauren grumbled as they went down the corridor towards the Bonds' flat. 'Thank goodness she doesn't know Mia's carrying Dillon around in her bag! Can you imagine her face if he'd popped his head out?'

Jas, Becky and Mia giggled.

'She's such a busy-body,' Lauren went on. 'Some day I'm going to walk right up to her and tell her to leave us alone—'

'Ssh, she just got out of the lift again and she's right behind us!' Jas hissed in Lauren's ear.

With a horrified gasp, Lauren whipped round. But the corridor was empty. Jas, Mia and Becky collapsed in hysterics.

'Jas, you big fat liar!' Lauren squealed, her shoulders sagging with relief.

Jas was almost helpless with laughter as

Lauren grabbed her arm and gave her a shake. 'Serves you right for not telling us the secret!' she gasped through her giggles.

'Maybe I won't now,' Lauren teased, unlocking the flat door. Her bedroom was just inside the front door, off the hallway, and she led the girls inside.

'Yes, I can see now that a tidy bedroom definitely *isn't* the surprise,' Becky remarked, looking around at the unmade bed, the clothes piled everywhere and the untidy heaps of CDs, books and magazines on the desk around the computer.

'Don't let Dillon out of your bag, Mia,' Jas advised as she stepped over a pile of books lying on the floor. 'You'll never find him again in here.'

'Well, we *could* spend some time tidying up and I'll tell you my news when we've finished,' Lauren suggested breezily, plonking herself down on her rumpled duvet. 'It'll probably take three or four hours to get everything sorted, but I'm *sure* you won't mind waiting that long—'

With a blood-curdling shriek of frustration, Jas rushed over and leaped on Lauren. Becky joined her and so did Mia, after placing her bag carefully on the desk.

'Tell us now, Lols!' Jas begged, bouncing up

and down on the bed. 'I can't wait a minute longer!'

Lauren laughed. 'OK, here goes!' She took a deep breath, but then stopped and frowned. 'What's that noise?'

'Oh, just stop it, Lauren, and tell us the secret!' Jas groaned. But Lauren put her finger to her lips. She tiptoed across the room and suddenly yanked open the bedroom door. Two boys fell into the bedroom with yelps of surprise.

'*Charlie!*' Lauren glared at her younger brother. 'How many times have I told you not to sneak around listening at my bedroom door?'

'But that's what secret agents do!' Charlie complained, climbing to his feet. He had curly auburn hair, big blue eyes and a smattering of freckles across his nose. 'We *have* to know what's going on.'

'Yes, so we can be ready to spring into action,' added Joe, Charlie's best friend.

Jas, Becky and Mia started laughing, but Lauren rolled her eyes.

'Just because your surname is Bond, Charlie, it doesn't mean you're a secret agent!' she pointed out. Her brother and his friend were obsessed with playing spies, and Charlie had even been known to go up to guests and introduce himself with the line, *My name's Bond, Charles Bond.* 'And anyway, spies shouldn't make any noise so you ought to go away and practise being quiet. I heard you outside the bedroom door just now!'

Charlie and Joe tiptoed off, talking to each other in whispers. Lauren closed the door again, pulling a face at the others.

'I wonder what that pair are plotting now.' Then she grinned as she spotted the look on Jas's face. 'Oh, yes, I've got something to tell you, haven't I! Well, there's a very, *very* special guest arriving at the hotel next Tuesday . . .'

Wide-eyed with anticipation, Jas, Mia and Becky stared at Lauren. Plenty of famous people had stayed at the hotel before, and the girls had even met some of them, but they could tell from the look of excitement on Lauren's face that this guest was extra-special.

'Who?' Jas breathed.

Lauren grinned from ear to ear. 'ISABELLA DUVAL!' she announced.

There was a stunned silence.

'Isabella Duval?' Jas repeated, dazed. 'Our favourite actress, Isabella Duval? Coming to the hotel? *The* Isabella Duval?'

'Yep!' Lauren nodded, enjoying the amazed

looks on her friends' faces. 'The one and only world-famous actress Isabella Duval is going to be staying right here at the Mayfair Park. Now *that* was worth waiting for, wasn't it?' She glanced at Becky, who was so shocked, she was speechless. All the girls loved Isabella Duval, but Lauren knew that Becky in particular was a *massive* fan of the actress. 'Say something, Becks,' Lauren went on. 'You look like you're about to faint!'

'I *feel* faint!' Becky squeaked, almost unable to get the words out. 'Why is Isabella Duval staying here? Is she on holiday or something?'

Lauren shook her head. 'Mum and Dad told me this morning that she's in London for five days to launch a new collection for Kaspari – you know, the *really* expensive Italian jewellers? They're exhibiting the collection at a gallery, and I think Isabella is going to model some of the jewellery.'

'Oh, I *loved* Isabella in *Where Two Rivers Meet*, and that film about the twin sisters where she played a double role,' Mia said. 'She was fab! Didn't she get nominated for an Oscar for that?'

Becky nodded. 'Do you think we'll get to meet her, Lols?'

'I don't know,' Lauren admitted. 'She's staying in the Ruby Suite on the top floor, and she might just want to be left alone – you know how some superstars are!'

'Well, wouldn't it be *brilliant* fun to try and come up with a top-secret plan to get to meet Isabella?' Mia suggested with a grin. 'That would be a bit of a challenge!'

Becky jumped off the bed and began to pace up and down the room.

'I *have* to meet Isabella and get her autograph!' she declared. 'There's *got* to be a way . . .'

There was silence for a moment and then Jas also leaped to her feet.

'I've got a plan for that,' she announced.

'Jas, you've always got a plan for *everything*!' Lauren said, smiling. 'It had better be a good one, though, because if it all goes wrong, I'll be grounded for life by Mum and Dad, and The Snoop will be thrilled!'

'Nooo!' Jas shook her head. 'That won't happen. This is foolproof – well, almost!'

'Tell us then, Jas,' Becky said eagerly.

'Right!' Jas began. 'This is what we'll do . . .'

CHAPTER TWO

Clutching her phone in one hand, Becky loitered just inside the hotel entrance, trying to make herself look as small and insignificant as possible. She was breathless with excitement and her heart was hammering like crazy. It was Tuesday afternoon, and the girls had rushed home from school to put their plan to meet Isabella Duval into action.

Becky peeped through the glass doors at the scene outside the hotel. There was a crowd of photographers waiting in a roped-off area, as well as a group of fans who'd obviously found out somehow that Isabella was arriving today. James, the hotel doorman, was also waiting attentively for Isabella's car to appear.

'That's brilliant, Jas,' Becky had said approvingly when Jas had finished outlining her plan. 'But it'll have to be organized to the very *second* if it's going to work.'

'Well, if anyone can do that, you can, Becks,' Jas had pointed out. 'It'll be more like a military operation! But don't forget this is supposed to be fun too . . .'

Since Saturday, Becky had gone through the plan in her head over and over again, day and night. It *seemed* pretty foolproof. Jas had reminded the girls that whenever a guest stayed in the luxury Ruby, Diamond, Sapphire or Emerald suites on the top floor of the hotel, Lauren's dad always sent up a welcome drink just after they'd checked in.

'So how about if *we* take an *unofficial* drink up to Isabella before the *real* one arrives?' Jas had suggested, her dark eyes dancing with glee.

'Great idea,' Mia had agreed. 'But we'll have to time it perfectly in order to get there before the bar staff do.'

'We can do that,' Becky had said confidently. 'But we need to make sure no one guesses what we're up to, so that Lauren doesn't get into any trouble.'

'Thanks, guys,' Lauren had said gratefully. 'I can just imagine The Snoop's face if she found out what we were plotting!'

Impatiently Becky peered out through the glass doors again, but there was still no sign of

Isabella's car. Suddenly, though, she saw Lauren's dad come out of his office, straightening his tie. Becky slipped discreetly out of sight behind a large potted palm, and her heart began to thump even harder as Mr Bond hurried over to the hotel doors. He'd obviously had a message to say that Isabella Duval was on her way . . .

A few moments later, a sleek black limo drew up outside the hotel steps, and the fans erupted into loud cheers and whoops. Becky felt so excited, she couldn't stop her knees from shaking. She edged out slightly from behind the palm and fixed her gaze on the car.

James had opened the door and was helping Isabella Duval out. Becky caught her breath as she got her first glimpse of the world-famous star. Isabella was very slender and slight, and was somewhat shorter in real life than she looked on-screen, Becky realized. But she was just as beautiful, with her very long, very dark hair and her tanned, golden skin. She wore a floaty maxi-dress in shades of pink and lilac and very high-heeled, strappy, pale lilac shoes. She looked stunning, Becky thought dreamily.

Isabella smiled warmly as she posed on the steps for pictures. There were more cheers from the fans, who were now waving their autograph books, trying to attract Isabella's attention, while the photographers' flashguns blazed away as they shot picture after picture of the star. As Lauren's dad hurried forward to welcome the actress and her companion, a man in a dark-grey suit, Becky gave herself a mental shake. This was it! Time to put their plan into action . . .

Mr Bond was now escorting Isabella up the steps to the hotel doors, the actress stopping to sign autographs along the way. As James opened the glass doors to admit them, Becky hit a button on her mobile to call Lauren. Now it was up to Lauren and Jas to sort out the next phase of the plan, Becky thought, peeping out from behind the palm to get a closer look at Isabella as she passed by . . .

'Right, Jas, Becky's just buzzed me,' Lauren whispered. 'Here we go!'

The two of them were sitting at a table in the hotel café-bar, which was empty at the moment apart from Kyle, the bar manager, who was polishing glasses behind the counter. There had been a few guests in there a little earlier, but they'd all gone out into reception to watch Isabella arrive. *Which is perfect for our plan*, Lauren thought, relieved.

'OK, leave this to me,' Jas whispered back. 'Ready, Lauren?'

Lauren nodded. Jas cleared her throat and stood up, pushing her chair back.

'Oh!' Jas gave a little scream. 'Kyle, Kyle, come quick!'

'What is it, Jas?' Kyle ran out from behind the bar, dropping the cloth he was holding.

'I saw an absolutely massive ginormous spider running along the wall over there!' Jas wailed, pointing at the far end of the café-bar.

Kyle grabbed a beer glass and coaster and rushed over. 'Where did it go?' he asked Jas. 'I'll trap it in this glass and put it outside.'

'I think it ran under that table,' Jas told him, pointing to the very far end of the café-bar. 'You *have* to catch it, Kyle, or the guests will freak out when they see it!'

While Kyle and Jas went to search for the non-existent gigantic spider, Lauren immediately ducked behind the counter and grabbed a silver tray. Quickly she opened the fridge behind the bar. Becky had spent hours on her computer Googling to find out Isabella's favourite drink, and had finally come up with the answer – pink champagne.

The bottom of the fridge was full of

mini-bottles of champagne. Carefully Lauren got one out and whipped off the foil top. She twisted the stopper out carefully, and then checked over her shoulder. Jas now had Kyle crawling around on the floor, looking for the imaginary spider. Trying not to giggle, Lauren took down a tall crystal champagne flute, placed it on the tray and filled it almost to the brim with the pale pink bubbly liquid.

'What are you doing?' asked a curious voice behind her.

Lauren jumped guiltily, almost spilling the champagne. She hadn't heard Charlie come into the bar, and now he was standing there staring at her.

'Nothing!' Lauren spluttered. At the other end of the café-bar, Jas had just glanced round, and was miming frantic 'hurry up' gestures at Lauren. They didn't have much time . . .

'I want to know,' Charlie insisted, his eyes mischievous. 'Tell me or I'll tell Kyle you're stealing champagne!'

'Look, it's for Isabella Duval, the actress in the Ruby Suite,' Lauren hissed quickly. 'We want to get to meet her, that's all.' Suddenly she had a brainwave. 'Anyway, listen, I've got a secret mission for you!'

Charlie's eyes widened. 'What is it?' he asked eagerly.

'Find me a white rose to put on the tray,' Lauren told him. 'It has to be a white rose, because they're Isabella's favourite flowers.'

'I'm on the case!' Charlie promised solemnly, and he dashed off. With a sigh of relief, Lauren picked up the tray and slipped out of the café-bar into the hotel lounge next door, which was thankfully pretty empty.

'Sorry, Kyle, maybe I was just imagining things,' Lauren heard Jas call apologetically. Then Jas came skipping out of the café-bar and joined Lauren in the lounge.

'Great stuff, Lauren!' Jas gasped with a huge grin. 'Everything's working brilliantly so far.'

At that moment Becky rushed in, phone in hand.

'You two are stars!' she exclaimed, thrilled when she saw the champagne. 'I've just seen Isabella, and she's gorgeous! She's on her way up to the Ruby Suite with Lauren's dad right now, so I'm just going to buzz Mia to let her know.'

'So far, so good!' Lauren laughed. 'Now it's all down to Mia . . .'

On the top floor of the hotel, Mia was lurking

around the lifts, phone in hand. The plan was that Becky would buzz her as soon as she saw Isabella leaving reception and getting into the lift on the way to her suite. A couple of the hotel porters had already arrived with Isabella's designer luggage and had placed it in her rooms, so Mia knew the star couldn't be far behind . . .

Mia peeped into her bag to check on Dillon. She was relieved to see that he'd eaten some of the seeds and was now fast asleep. The gerbil had been off his food for a few days, and Mia had almost decided to take him to the vet, but it looked like he was getting better all on his own. Mia felt very relieved. She hated to see an animal under the weather.

Suddenly Mia almost leaped out of her skin as her phone buzzed. Quickly she hit the STOP button and then scuttled out of sight behind a mahogany bookcase that stood in the corridor. Isabella was on her way!

A few moments later Mia heard the lift doors open and the sound of footsteps.

'And if there's anything you want or need, Miss Duval, anything at all,' Lauren's dad was saying, 'please don't hesitate to let us know.'

'Thank you, Mr Bond,' Isabella replied, 'that's very kind.' Mia felt a thrill run down her spine as she heard the actress's familiar tones. She longed to take a peep at Isabella but it might ruin their whole plan, so she restrained herself.

Mia waited silently behind the bookcase as she heard Lauren's dad unlock the suite and show Isabella in. A few moments later he came out, and this time Mia risked a quick peep. She saw the lift doors close as Mr Bond left the top floor and went downstairs again.

With a huge sigh of relief, Mia quickly buzzed her friends' phones. All she had to do now was hope that the other girls were on their way . . .

As Lauren and the others waited in the lounge for Mia's signal, Charlie sidled into the room, glancing left and right as if he thought he was being followed.

'What's *he* doing here?' Jas whispered as Charlie hurried over to them.

'I sent him on a mission to get him out of the way!' Lauren explained.

'Here's your flower.' Charlie produced a white rose from behind his back. 'I took it from the display on the reception desk, but don't worry' – he looked very proud of himself – 'nobody saw me.'

'Good work, Mr Bond!' Lauren said, winking

at Jas and Becky as she laid the rose carefully on the tray. 'I suppose you'd better come with us and meet Isabella, then.'

Charlie didn't look very impressed. 'I don't know who she is,' he said with a shrug. 'I haven't seen any of her films. Has she ever played a spy?'

'I don't think so,' replied Becky.

'What about an evil scientist then?'

'Nope,' Jas told him.

'An SAS soldier?'

Jas, Becky and Lauren shook their heads.

'Oh.' Charlie yawned. 'She sounds really boring. I won't bother. I've got better things to do.' And, nicking a couple of apples from the large bowl of fruit on the coffee table, he began trying to juggle with them.

The three girls glanced at each other and laughed, but they stopped abruptly as all three of their phones began to buzz, one after the other.

'That's Mia's signal,' Becky said breathlessly. 'Let's go for it!'

Leaving Charlie chasing the apples he'd dropped, Becky, Lauren and Jas hurried off to the lifts. They waited for an empty one to come along and then slipped inside. The girls stood silently as the lift glided towards the top floor,

Lauren still holding the tray. Becky hardly dared to breathe, she was so worried. She felt hot with embarrassment and fear at the thought that someone like The Snoop might get into the lift and then they'd have to explain why they were carrying a glass of champagne on a tray ... Becky fixed her eyes on the display of floor numbers above the door, willing them to keep moving upwards.

At last there was a *ping* as the lift reached the tenth floor. Becky heaved a huge, shaky sigh of relief as the doors slid open and they stepped out to find Mia waiting for them.

'Oh, you got the champagne, guys!' Mia exclaimed. 'Well done, you.'

'The plan's worked beautifully so far, Mia,' Becky confided. 'Did you catch a glimpse of Isabella? She is so beautiful!'

Mia shook her head regretfully.

'Lauren and I haven't seen her yet either,' Jas said, whipping out a brush and smoothing down her hair. 'We can't wait! Hey, has anyone got any lip-gloss?'

'I have.' Becky pulled a tube of strawberry-flavoured gloss out of her pocket. She handed it round and the girls tidied themselves up, brushing their hair and applying the lip-gloss. Even

Lauren, who hardly ever wore make-up, put a slick of gloss on.

'Right!' Becky said with a nervous gulp, wishing her knees would stop knocking together. 'Let's do this, guys . . .'

Lauren picked up the tray again and the girls tiptoed over to the door of the Ruby Suite.

'Why are we tiptoeing?' Jas whispered.

'And why are we whispering?' Mia asked.

'Because we're incredibly nervous!' Becky replied in a low voice. 'Well, I am, anyway . . .' She stopped outside Isabella's door and stared at it, but made no move to ring the bell. *Isabella Duval is behind that very door*, Becky thought, her heart racing. She was so scared and excited, she didn't know what to do.

'I realize this suggestion might be a bit out-there,' Jas remarked, 'but shouldn't you ring the bell, Becky?'

'I can't!' Becky wailed, trying to quell the butterflies swooping around inside her tummy. 'I'm too nervous.'

Jas patted her comfortingly on the shoulder. 'Look, Becky, we've done the hard bit,' she pointed out. 'If you won't, I will!' And reaching out, she pushed the bell.

'Isabella's probably tired after her flight from

the States,' Becky gabbled nervously. 'We'll just hand over the drink and leave.'

'I thought you'd brought your *Where Two Rivers Meet* DVD for Isabella to sign?' Lauren reminded her friend.

'I have,' Becky mumbled, 'but I don't want to bother her.'

'I'll ask for you, then,' Jas said in her usual direct manner.

'Ssh!' Mia hissed. 'Someone's coming!'

Becky could hardly contain her excitement as the door opened. There was Isabella Duval herself, standing right in front of them.

'Hello?' Isabella said enquiringly, smiling at them.

Becky knew she was staring. She also knew that her mouth had fallen open, but she couldn't help it. She was completely star-struck! Even Jas, who always had a comment for every occasion, was speechless.

Isabella was still smiling. 'Is that for me?' she asked, pointing at the glass of champagne.

'Er – yes,' Lauren stammered. 'It's a welcome drink, compliments of the hotel management.'

'We know it's your favourite, Miss Duval,' Jas added, finally finding her voice.

'Oh, how kind,' Isabella said, her almond-shaped eyes twinkling. 'You're right, pink champagne *is* my favourite drink! Thank you so much.'

'Um, Miss Duval, would you mind signing my mate Becky's DVD for her?' Jas asked, sounding quite shy for once as she nodded at Becky. 'We're all big fans of yours, but Becky's your biggest fan *ever*!'

Becky blushed as Isabella smiled directly at her.

'Of course I will.' Isabella opened the door wider. 'Do come in, girls. And please call me Isabella.'

Hardly able to believe their luck, the girls walked into the huge luxury Ruby Suite. The living-room was full of antique furniture and dark-red leather sofas, with oil paintings and gilt-framed mirrors on the walls. Beautiful displays of exotic red orchids were positioned carefully here and there. Off the living-room, other doors stood ajar. Through one of them, the girls could see an enormous bedroom with a four-poster bed draped with deep red silk curtains trimmed with gold fringes, and through another, a spectacular bathroom of chrome, marble and glass.

'That bathroom's bigger than the whole of my house!' Jas whispered jokingly to Becky.

'I've never stayed at the Mayfair Park before, but I love it already,' Isabella declared as Lauren put the tray carefully down on the coffee-table. She glanced around the living-room. 'This is one of the nicest suites I've ever stayed in. I adore the red décor.'

'There are three other suites called the Diamond, Emerald and Sapphire suites,' Lauren explained. 'And they're all decorated in the gem-stone colours too.'

'Well, I'm very glad I'm in the Ruby Suite because red is one of my very favourite colours. I think Kaspari booked it especially for me because I'm launching their new ruby collection. Wasn't that kind of them?' Isabella picked up the champagne glass and took a tiny sip. 'Thank you for making me feel so welcome, girls,' she went on. 'Now, where's this DVD you want me to sign, Becky?'

With a broad smile, Becky took the DVD out of her shoulder bag and handed it to Isabella. She was still a teeny bit nervous, but Isabella was so natural, warm and friendly that Becky was feeling much more relaxed.

To Becky, my biggest fan! Isabella wrote with a flourish. *Lovely to meet you. Best wishes, Isabella Duval.*

'Thank you!' Becky gasped.

'You're very welcome,' Isabella declared, taking another sip of champagne. 'So, tell me, girls, how are you connected to the hotel?'

'I'm Lauren, and my dad, Mr Bond, is the manager,' Lauren explained. 'Jas, Mia and Becky are my best friends.'

'Oh, Lauren, please do tell your father how much I *love* my suite,' Isabella said enthusiastically. 'There's only *one* thing missing . . .'

'What's that?' Mia asked shyly.

'A tub of double chocolate fudge ice-cream,' Isabella replied.

Becky and the others stared at her in surprise and then began to laugh.

'I know, isn't it shocking?' Isabella sighed, her face breaking into a smile. 'Double chocolate fudge ice-cream is my favourite thing *ever*, and I eat far too much of it. So I guess it's probably a good thing that there isn't any!'

'I'll ask my dad to send some up,' Lauren promised, as there was a knock at the door.

'That will be Max,' Isabella guessed, hurrying to open it. A tall, dark-haired man in a grey suit stood outside, holding a silver box in his arms, and Becky recognized him immediately as the man who'd arrived in the limo with Isabella earlier.

'Ooh, my shoes!' Isabella squealed excitedly, taking the box from him. 'Girls, this is my PA, Max Carroll. Max, meet my new friends, Becky, Jas, Mia and Lauren.'

'Delighted to meet you, girls,' Max said smoothly, nodding at them. 'Any friends of Isabella's are definitely friends of mine.'

Becky smiled politely at him, but secretly she couldn't help thinking that Max was *just* a little bit smarmy. There was something about his slicked-back hair, dazzlingly white teeth and general manner that she just didn't warm to. She glanced at Jas, who pulled a quick face at her, and Becky guessed she was thinking the same thing.

Meanwhile Isabella had put the box on the bed, and was eagerly unwrapping swathes of the palest pink tissue paper. Then, with a cry of delight, she pulled out a pair of glittering, ruby-red shoes with twinkling crystal stiletto heels.

'Oh!' Becky breathed. 'They are just *gorgeous*!'

'I've never seen anything so sparkly,' Jas sighed enviously, staring at the shimmering heels. 'You'll look like you're walking on light, Isabella!'

'They're to go with my dress for the Kaspari

jewellery launch,' Isabella confided, turning the shoes this way and that to admire them. 'Are you sure they're the right size for me, Max?'

Max nodded. 'Size three. But maybe you'd better try them on, just to be sure.'

'*I'm* a size three too!' Becky blurted out. Then she blushed as the others smiled.

'Would you like to try them on, Becky?' Isabella asked, holding out the sparkling ruby shoes.

Becky was so excited, she could hardly kick her flip-flops off fast enough. She took the shoes from Isabella, handling them as carefully as if they were made of glass, and then slipped one onto her right foot. She tried to stand on one leg to put the other shoe on, but the heels were so high, she wobbled a little and had to hang on to Jas.

'They look fabulous!' Mia said, eyes wide.

Becky tried to take a few steps, but now she began wobbling about even more on the glittering, skyscraper heels, and with a grin, she collapsed onto one of the sofas.

'They're beautiful but too high for me!' Becky said, handing the shoes back to Isabella.

'Oh, I *love* high heels,' Isabella told her. 'I'm so short, I've always worn them and so I can walk for miles in them now. Just don't ask me to run the London Marathon in heels, that's all!' She put her hand on Max's shoulder to steady herself as she slipped the shoes on. 'Look! I can actually talk to Max face to face when I'm wearing these,' Isabella said with a huge smile. In the ruby shoes, she was now as tall as he was, Becky could see. 'Usually I only come up to his shoulder!'

'What outfit are you wearing with the shoes, Isabella?' Lauren asked curiously.

Isabella whisked across the room, crystal heels twinkling in the light, and unzipped a clothes bag lying on one of the sofas. Then carefully she took out a long red velvet gown with a square neckline, nipped-in waist and flowing skirt.

'Oh, you'll look so beautiful!' Becky exclaimed, wishing that there was some way she and the other girls could go to the jewellery exhibition and see Isabella launch the new collection in her gorgeous dress and glittering shoes.

'Thank you,' Isabella replied, looking pleased as she zipped the dress into the bag again.

'Maybe we should go now,' Mia whispered to Becky. 'Isabella must be tired.'

Becky nodded. 'We'll leave you to rest now,

Isabella,' she said. A look of relief flashed across Max's face, Becky noticed, but it was gone so quickly, she wasn't sure if she'd imagined it. 'It was lovely to meet you. Thank you *so* much for the autograph.'

'And thank you for showing us your lovely shoes,' said Jas gratefully.

'*And* your dress,' Mia added.

'I won't forget to ask my dad about the double chocolate fudge ice-cream too!' Lauren told her.

'It was lovely to meet you, girls,' Isabella said warmly as she saw them to the door. 'I do hope we meet again before I leave.' She sounded as if she *really* meant it too, Becky thought. 'Bye for now . . .'

'Was that a dream or did I *really* meet Isabella Duval?' Becky murmured as, with a friendly wave, Isabella closed the door behind them.

'Well, if it *was* a dream, I was having the exact same one!' Jas laughed. 'Wasn't Isabella *lovely*? I can't believe how nice she was.'

'Yes, she must meet hundreds of new people every day, and she even remembered our names,' Lauren marvelled.

'She doesn't act a bit like a star,' said Mia as

the four of them headed off down the corridor, 'and she *must* be one of the most famous people in the world!'

Just before they reached the lifts, the door opened. Becky's eyes widened as she saw Kyle, the bar manager, step out of the lift, carrying a glass of champagne on a silver tray. She glanced at Mia, Jas and Lauren and the four of them exchanged a huge grin.

'Here comes Isabella's *official* welcome drink,' Becky murmured. 'Time to make a run for it, girls!'

CHAPTER THREE

'Let's start by Googling *Kaspari's new collection*,' Jas suggested, squeezing onto a corner of Mia's chair as the four of them gathered around the classroom computer.

Mia nodded, her fingers flying across the keyboard. Jas watched her admiringly, wishing she could type that fast herself. But Mia was a PC ace, thanks to her two older brothers, who were computer geeks.

'Look, there are *heaps* of links,' Becky pointed out as the page loaded.

'That's because there's been so much publicity about it ever since Isabella arrived,' replied Lauren.

It was Wednesday, the day after the girls had met Isabella, and following the official announcement that the actress was in town to launch the new Kaspari collection, there'd been a huge media frenzy to secure pictures and

interviews with her, as well as advance information about the collection. Isabella and the
jewellery launch were all over the TV, radio,
newspapers and celebrity magazines.

Today the girls had been thrilled when their
Media Studies teacher at school, Miss Greene,
had started off a discussion in class about Isabella
Duval and the Kaspari collection. The other
students had listened, fascinated, as Lauren, Jas,
Mia and Becky told them how they'd met the
star when she arrived at the Mayfair Park. That
had led onto a discussion about the advantages
and disadvantages of celebrities being involved
in advertising and launching new products, and
then Miss Greene had given each group a project
to research.

'Isn't Miss Greene just the *coolest* Media
Studies teacher *ever*?' Jas remarked as Mia clicked
on one of the Google links. 'I could have given
her a great big hug when she said our project was
to find out about Isabella and the new Kaspari
collection.'

'Go on then, I dare you!' Lauren said mis-
chievously, glancing at the teacher, who was
chatting with another group. Jas laughed and
poked her tongue out at Lauren.

'This looks interesting.' Mia had clicked on

one of the links, the website of a national newspaper, and now she read out one of the front-page headlines. *'Kaspari collection inspired by legendary ancient ruby.'*

'Wow!' Becky exclaimed, staring at the colour photo in front of them. 'That is *totally* amazing.'

The girls gazed at the screen in silent wonder. Jas thought she'd never seen such a *stunning* piece of jewellery anywhere, ever. The gold necklace was curved like a collar to fit around the neck, and its shining surface was delicately hammered and engraved to create swirling, intricate patterns. But what really drew the eye was the large ruby hanging from the middle of the necklace. It was teardrop-shaped, and the ruby-red colour was so deep and intense and clear that Jas was mesmerized by it.

'Listen to this,' said Mia, beginning to read from the article. *'The teardrop ruby is one of the most beautiful, perfectly formed and valuable stones in the whole world. Legend has it that Cleopatra, the famous queen of ancient Egypt, was wearing the golden necklace when she died, and that the teardrop ruby was formed from the drop of blood that fell after she was bitten by the asp that killed her. The ruby necklace is now owned by an American museum which has agreed to loan it to Kaspari for the launch.'*

'Awesome!' Lauren's eyes were as big as saucers. 'Maybe the Cleopatra bit isn't totally true, but what an *amazing* story.'

'Can somebody *please* tell me what an asp is?' Becky asked.

Mia had printed out the picture of the necklace and was now Googling busily again. 'It's a small, poisonous snake,' she replied.

Jas picked up the print-out and stared at the necklace once more. If it really *was* as old as Cleopatra, it must have passed through many different hands before it ended up as the inspiration for the new Kaspari collection, she thought. What stories it could tell, if only it could speak . . . 'Are there any other legends about the necklace, Mia?' she asked.

'I think there are probably loads more,' Mia replied. 'We'll have to research them thoroughly for our project. But take a look at this . . .' She scrolled further down the article and read aloud: '*Over the years, there have been many rumours of plots to steal this priceless necklace, and whenever it is put on public display, there is always a massive security presence. The necklace will be exhibited at the Kaspari jewellery launch in the Columbine Gallery on Saturday, but the only time it will be allowed out of its special impregnable case is when top Hollywood*

actress Isabella Duval, the face of Kaspari's new col-
lection, wears it for a media photo-call at the launch.'

'The necklace will look gorgeous with Isabella's velvet dress and ruby-red crystal shoes,' Becky sighed. 'I wish we could see it.'

'We could wait in reception for her to leave for the launch,' Jas pointed out. 'At least we'd get a glimpse of *her* then.'

'And the Columbine Gallery is only round the corner from the hotel,' Lauren said eagerly. 'We could go there and watch Isabella arrive.'

'And maybe we could get a photo of Isabella in her outfit,' Mia suggested. 'Then we could add it to our project. She might even give us an inter-view too, if we ask nicely.'

'That's a totally fabulous idea,' Jas agreed. 'I bet she wouldn't mind at all. Mia, are there any pictures of the new jewellery collection that we can put in our project too?'

Mia shook her head. 'I think the collection itself is being kept top secret until the actual launch,' she said, flipping backwards and forwards through some of the links.

'I wonder if there's a brochure or a leaflet about the launch that we can get hold of,' Becky suggested. 'It might have pictures of the collection.'

Jas frowned, disappointed. But then she had an idea . . .

'The *best* thing would be if we could actually go to the launch and *see* the collection for ourselves,' Jas said eagerly. 'And you know what—?'

'Jas!' Lauren groaned, rolling her eyes. 'You can't *possibly* have a plan for that.'

'No, I haven't – yet,' Jas admitted. 'But I'm working on it, guys!'

Lauren invited the girls over after school for a swim in the hotel pool. As usual, Jas turned up first, and she and Lauren had decided to go down and get changed while they waited for Becky and Mia to arrive.

'Have you seen Isabella again, Lols?' Jas asked as the two of them left the Bonds' flat and headed towards the staff lift.

'No, not a glimpse,' Lauren sighed as they walked down the corridor. 'She's been out all the time, doing interviews, and rehearsing for the launch, I guess. Any ideas yet on how we're going to get in and see the collection for ourselves?'

'I thought we could dress up as Egyptian princesses, claim we're descendants of Cleopatra and try to talk our way in,' Jas suggested. 'What do you think?'

'I think – not a hope!' Lauren retorted.

'My *other* plan is that maybe, just maybe, we could drop a teeny-tiny hint to Isabella about getting us four complimentary tickets,' Jas went on.

'Mm, that's *better*,' Lauren said thoughtfully. 'But I'd be *so* dead if my dad found out! He'd be totally non-impressed if he thought we were bothering Isabella for tickets.'

'OK, maybe dressing up as Egyptian princesses *is* our best bet, after all,' Jas said with a grin. 'Do you think we can borrow an asp from somewhere?'

'Don't mention it to Mia – she could probably get one!' Lauren giggled.

As the girls stopped outside the lift, Charlie and Joe came sneaking down the corridor. Lauren raised her eyebrows when she saw that the two boys were each carrying a bucket.

'What are you up to?' she asked suspiciously.

'Secret agents never tell,' Charlie replied. 'Not even under torture!'

'They're probably on their way to play a trick on someone,' Lauren said to Jas as the boys hurried off.

Jas grinned. 'Well, let's hope The Snoop is the victim!'

The lift doors slid open, and Jas and Lauren walked in. One of the young chambermaids was already in there with a housekeeping trolley, piled high with clean sheets, pillowcases and towels. She looked fraught, and very miserable.

'Hi, Rachel, are you OK?' Lauren asked. 'You look a bit down.'

'I'm fine,' Rachel sighed, adjusting her spotless white apron. 'But I've been running around all day, and I'm *still* not finished yet. Mrs Stoop gave me loads of extra work, and I'm all behind.'

'Trust The Snoop!' Jas whispered in Lauren's ear. Jas and the others really liked Rachel, who was usually sunny and cheerful and always very friendly.

'Can Jas and I do anything to help?' Lauren asked. 'We're meeting Becky and Mia at the pool, but we've got a bit of time.'

'Oh! Would you?' Rachel brightened at once. 'I've been meaning to pop up to the ninth floor to give Mr Carroll, Miss Duval's PA, his dry cleaning, but I haven't had a minute.'

'We'll be happy to take it,' Jas said, giving Lauren a wink. She could see from her friend's face that Lauren had had the exact same thought as Jas – that Isabella *might* just be with Max!

Looking very relieved, Rachel handed over a couple of jackets in a dry-cleaning bag to Lauren.

'Thanks so much, girls,' she called gratefully as she pushed the trolley out onto the sixth floor. 'It's room nine-o-one. See you later.'

'I hope Isabella's there!' Lauren said, beaming at Jas as the lift glided up to the ninth floor. 'What did you think of Max, Jas? I thought he was a bit greasy and smarmy, to be honest.'

'Greasier than a plate of big, fat, greasy chips!' Jas replied solemnly, and Lauren laughed.

When they reached room 901, Jas knocked on the door.

'Come in,' they heard Max call.

Jas swung the door open and a big grin swept across her face. Isabella, looking dressed-down but gorgeous as ever in cut-off faded jeans and a white sleeveless T-shirt, was sitting on the bed. Her long hair was loose and her feet bare. Jas smiled at her, but was surprised when Isabella didn't respond.

Max, meanwhile, was standing at the desk, sifting through a pile of paperwork. 'And we really have to make sure that everything runs to time. It has to go like clockwork—' He broke off abruptly as Jas and Lauren walked in, and flashed them a distracted smile.

'Ah, my dry-cleaning. Thank you, girls. Would you hang it on the back of the door, please?'

Jas helped Lauren to hang the jackets on a hook behind the door. She was hoping that Isabella would say something to them, but the actress remained completely silent. However, Jas was determined not to lose this chance to speak to Isabella again, so she turned round and gave her another big smile.

'How are you today, Isabella?' she asked politely.

Isabella's beautiful face broke into a scowl. 'That's *Miss Duval* to you,' she retorted haughtily, raising a perfectly arched eyebrow. 'And since you ask, I'm having *the* worst day!' And she directed her scowl at Max, who was looking rather uncomfortable.

'Maybe some double chocolate fudge ice-cream would help?' Lauren suggested.

Isabella stared at Lauren as if she was crazy. 'What are you talking about?' she demanded angrily. 'I don't even *like* ice-cream. Now please go away and stop bothering me, or I'll complain to the hotel manager.'

The girls exchanged bewildered glances. Jas

could hardly believe her ears. Isabella Duval seemed to have changed completely in just a day or so. And not for the better, either . . .

'Sorry, girls,' Max said smoothly, hurrying across the room towards them. 'As you can probably imagine, Isabella's very tired and stressed after all the preparations for the launch. She'll be happy to chat to you later, but would you mind excusing us just now, please?' And politely he escorted Jas and Lauren out.

But just before he closed the door behind them, Jas heard Max say impatiently to Isabella: 'For goodness' sake, you're going to have to do better than that! Just try to be more polite, and don't make this situation any more difficult than it already is . . .'

Jas turned to Lauren.

'Did you hear that?' she whispered.

Lauren nodded. 'What's going on, Jas?' she whispered back. 'This is weird! One minute Isabella likes double chocolate fudge ice-cream, the next minute she can't stand it!'

Jas sighed. 'I guess Isabella isn't as nice as we thought,' she replied. 'She's a bit of a superstar diva all right!'

Lauren pulled a face. 'I know. Becky'll be a bit disappointed when we tell her.'

Still discussing Isabella's strange behaviour, Jas and Lauren headed for the hotel pool on the ground floor. It was an enormous blue and white tiled room with a large domed roof. There were sun-loungers lying around the poolside, and tall palms in terracotta pots, and there was also a bubbling Jacuzzi, a sauna and a steam room. Glass doors at one the side of the pool led into the hotel spa.

Becky and Mia were already swimming up and down the Olympic-sized pool. They waved at Lauren and Jas, who ran to change, and then joined them in the warm water.

'Where've you two been?' Mia asked, swimming up to Jas, who'd just dived in neatly with barely a splash. 'Becky and I thought you'd be here before us.'

Jas glanced at Lauren. 'Well, we were on our way down here and then we met Rachel, and she was upset because The Snoop had given her loads of work—'

'Oh, The Snoop is *always* mean to Rachel,' Becky said with a frown. 'It makes me so *mad*.'

'So we offered to help out, and Rachel gave us Max's dry-cleaning to take to him,' Lauren went on.

Becky was so excited, she stopped swimming

and almost sank. 'Was Isabella there?' she spluttered through a mouthful of water.

'Yes, she was, but listen to *this*!' Jas exclaimed.

She told Mia and Becky exactly what had happened earlier in Max's room, Lauren chipping in with extra details now and then. Jas saw Becky's face drop as they explained how rude Isabella had been to them.

'I did think Isabella couldn't *possibly* be that nice all the time,' Becky said when Jas had finished. 'I mean, she's a superstar, and everyone knows how difficult they can be!'

'What a diva,' Mia commented.

'Oh, well, I don't think I'll be asking Isabella for any tickets to the jewellery launch now,' Jas said with a shrug. 'She threatened to report Lauren to her own dad for offering her ice-cream, so she'd probably have me arrested if I asked for tickets!'

'Max tried to cover for her, though,' Lauren added. 'He said Isabella was tired and stressed because of the launch coming up.'

'I know, he was being extra-nice to us, wasn't he, Lols?' Jas agreed. 'But I still don't like him much!'

'Neither do I,' Mia agreed. 'And I noticed that when we were in Isabella's room the other day,

Dillon was running around inside my bag, getting agitated whenever he heard Max's voice.' She stared solemnly at the others. 'Animals have a sixth sense about people, you know – and Dillon *definitely* doesn't like Max!'

'I'm with Dillon,' Becky remarked. 'Max is just too smarmy and smooth.'

'Yes, there's something completely fake about him,' Jas said thoughtfully. 'I get the feeling Max Carroll isn't all he seems . . .'

CHAPTER FOUR

'Look, there's Max,' Becky whispered as she, Jas and Mia came out of the lift into reception. The three girls were on their way home a little later that same evening, having said their goodbyes to Lauren. 'He's just coming out of the restaurant.'

Max Carroll was now standing near the glass doors that led out of the hotel, punching a number into his sleek silver phone. Jas pulled a face as she turned to Mia and Becky.

'Quick, let's leave while he's not looking,' she said. 'We don't want to talk to him, do we?'

Becky and Mia shook their heads firmly. The girls hurried towards the doors, not looking at Max and hoping he didn't spot them.

'Oh, hello there.' Max didn't even look up from his phone as the girls rushed past him. 'This is Chris.'

Becky was so shocked, she almost came to a dead stop. Had Max just introduced himself to someone as *Chris*, or was she hearing things? But when she glanced over at Jas and Mia, she could see that they were looking just as stunned.

'Am I dreaming, or did Max just say his name was Chris?' Jas whispered as Max walked off across the hotel lobby, still talking into his phone.

'We couldn't have misheard, could we?' Mia wondered with a frown. 'I mean, Chris sounds nothing like Max!'

Instead of leaving the hotel, the three girls paused by the doors, staring after Max as he strode off towards the lifts. Becky could tell that the conversation he was having was becoming more heated because Max was frowning, shrugging his shoulders and gesturing with his free hand as he talked. Who was he speaking to, and why on earth hadn't he told them his real name? It was a mystery, Becky thought, shaking her head in confusion.

Suddenly Max veered sharply to the left to avoid a group of people coming out of the café-bar. He was so intent on his phone conversation that he didn't see the small, slight figure of an elderly woman directly ahead of him. Becky recognized her immediately as Mrs Lloyd, a wealthy guest who stayed at the hotel so often she almost lived there. The girls watched as Max crashed right into Mrs Lloyd and accidentally knocked her expensive leather handbag out of her hand. The bag burst open as it hit the ground, and the contents tipped out all over the marble floor.

'Oh!' Mrs Lloyd gasped, looking very flustered. She bent over and grabbed her handbag, a diamond ring glittering on her finger as she began to scoop up her scattered possessions. 'I'm *so* sorry. How silly of me.'

'Why is Mrs Lloyd apologizing?' Jas whispered. 'It wasn't *her* fault.'

Looking annoyed and impatient, Max was helping Mrs Lloyd pick up her belongings. But Becky noticed that he stayed on his phone the whole time and he didn't say one word to the elderly guest. He didn't even apologize. Then, as soon as everything was safely back in the handbag, Max hurried off into one of the lifts without a backward glance.

'I think we were right about Max,' Jas said thoughtfully as the three of them left the hotel. 'He really *doesn't* seem very nice, does he?'

'And Dillon was running around again inside my bag as soon as he heard Max's voice!' Mia added.

'It is strange,' Lauren murmured. 'But I don't suppose Max is really up to anything dodgy.'

'Yes,' Becky agreed. 'There's probably some really simple explanation for the whole "Chris" thing . . .'

'Sorry I'm late, girls,' Lauren called apologetically as she dashed into the school playground the following morning. She looked like she'd just rolled straight out of bed and into her school uniform, Jas thought with a grin. Lauren's hair was sticking up all over her head and there were toast crumbs on her navy-blue sweatshirt. 'What a morning!'

'You'd better tidy yourself up a bit,' Jas said, handing over her comb and mirror. 'You look like you've just walked out of a tornado!'

'Oh, you don't know the half of it,' Lauren groaned. She took the comb, pulled a face at herself in the mirror and began smoothing her hair down. 'Mrs Lloyd says a gold watch of hers has gone missing. It's an antique, apparently, and it's *really* valuable.'

'Maybe she's just lost it,' Becky suggested.

Lauren shook her head. 'No, Mrs Lloyd's convinced it's been stolen. She was so upset, Dad called the police and the hotel's been put on security alert. Of course, Charlie's dead excited about it all! He says it's a new secret agent mission and he and Joe are going to track down the thief before the police do.'

'Do the police suspect anyone?' asked Mia.

Lauren sighed. 'From the questions they're asking, it looks like they think it might be one of the cleaning staff,' she replied. 'But we know them all really well, and Dad doesn't think it's any of them. Neither do I.'

Jas hadn't said anything much up until now, but that was because she was thinking furiously. Maybe it was a bit of a long shot, Jas decided at last, but it might be worth asking the other girls what they thought . . .

'Do you think *Max* might have had something to do with the theft of Mrs Lloyd's watch?' she burst out, unable to keep her suspicions to herself any longer.

Lauren, Mia and Becky turned to stare at her in complete shock, and for a moment Jas wished that she'd kept her mouth shut.

'Max?' Lauren repeated. 'You mean, Isabella's PA? Why would *he* be involved?'

Quickly Jas explained what had happened the night before in the hotel lobby.

'Mrs Lloyd might have been keeping the

watch in her handbag and Max would have had the perfect opportunity to nick it when he helped her collect up her stuff,' Jas went on. 'After all, we *did* hear him call himself Chris, so he might be up to *something*.'

'Yes, but calling yourself another name is a bit different from stealing a valuable antique,' Mia pointed out.

'And *Chris* could just be a nickname or something,' Lauren added. 'I mean, his surname is Carroll, so it could be a joke. You know, *Chris*tmas Carroll!'

'Oh.' Jas felt a bit deflated. 'I didn't think of that.'

'And why would Max steal it, anyway?' Becky said. 'What would he want with a woman's antique watch?'

'He could sell it for a pile of cash,' Jas argued.

Becky didn't look very convinced. 'Max wears designer suits and works for Isabella,' she replied. 'He must be *loaded*.'

'I bet Mrs Lloyd has just forgotten where she put the watch,' Lauren predicted confidently. 'It'll turn up somewhere, you'll see.'

Jas nodded, wishing she hadn't said anything about her suspicions of Max. Of course the other girls were right. Why on earth would someone who worked for one of the most famous Hollywood stars on the planet steal a watch from an elderly woman? It was ridiculous . . .

'Sorry, guys,' Jas said ruefully. 'Ignore me. I think I'm turning into a girlie version of Charlie and Joe!'

'Please, no!' Lauren begged. 'Don't do that to me!'

'You really don't like Max, do you, Jas?' Mia laughed as they headed into school for morning lessons.

Jas shook her head. 'Like I said before,' she replied, 'there's something about him that gives me the creeps. I just don't know what it is . . .'

'Look, here are some of the legends about the ruby necklace that I've found for our project,' Mia explained. She accessed the bookmarks on her laptop and a list of links flashed up onto the screen. 'There are a couple of brilliant stories here. One legend is that the necklace was once owned by a French princess, and she gave it to a poor sailor as a reward for saving her life when she was shipwrecked and almost drowned.'

'Awesome!' Becky breathed, her eyes round.

The girls had decided to get together after

school to work on their Media Studies project, and they were huddled around Mia's laptop at their favourite table in a corner of the hotel café-bar. The room was quiet and peaceful as there was no one around except Max, who was alone and working at his own laptop, and an elderly couple having afternoon tea. Mia could see Becky peering eagerly at the door every so often, obviously hoping that Isabella might come in and join Max. They hadn't even caught a glimpse of Isabella recently, as she'd been so busy preparing for the jewellery launch on Saturday.

'Here's another.' Mia clicked on the second link. 'There's a rumour that the necklace was once owned by an Italian count. He gambled it away in a game of cards, and then it went missing for over a hundred years. It was later found buried in the ground by a farmer who was ploughing his field.'

'This is all great stuff for our project,' Jas said with a grin. But Mia saw her glance surreptitiously across to the table near them where Max was sitting. He was studying the laptop screen intently, a cup of black coffee and his mobile phone beside him.

'Hey, we're supposed to be concentrating on

our project!' Mia whispered, giving Jas a gentle poke in the ribs.

Suddenly Max's phone rang, which made all four girls jump. They looked over and saw him snatch the phone off the table eagerly.

'Hello?' he said in a low voice. 'Yes, it's me.' He lowered his voice even more, and Mia couldn't hear everything he said. She just caught a few snippets. *No, trust me, it's safe . . . No, she's got no idea . . .*

Just then Max glanced over and saw the girls staring at him. Abruptly he jumped to his feet and hurried out of the café-bar to continue his conversation in private.

'Did you hear that?' Jas demanded, her eyes alight with excitement. *'No, trust me, it's safe. No, she's got no idea.* I bet he's talking about Mrs Lloyd's watch! I knew it was him – I just knew it!'

'You could be right, Jas,' Becky said slowly.

'It *does* sound suspicious, doesn't it?' Mia agreed.

'Yes, but we can't know for *sure* that's what Max is talking about,' Lauren pointed out with a frown.

'True . . .' Mia said thoughtfully. Then she grinned. 'But I have an idea! I'm just going to get some sugar from the counter . . .' And she stood up and wandered off towards Max's table.

As Mia passed by, she sneaked a quick look at the open laptop. But, annoyingly, the screensaver, a scene from one of Isabella's films, had popped up, replacing whatever Max had been looking at previously. Mia gave a silent sigh of frustration. But she wasn't defeated yet . . .

Mia collected a couple of sachets of sugar from the counter, smiled at Kyle, the bar manager, and headed back towards Max's table again. This time, as she passed by, she reached out casually and brushed her fingers quickly across the tracker pad. Instantly the screensaver faded away and the website Max had been viewing before his phone rang was revealed.

The Great Antiques Emporium – your place to buy and sell antiques online! Mia read silently. Her heart thudding with excitement, she hurried back to the others and told them what she'd seen.

'So Max is going to sell Mrs Lloyd's antique watch!' Jas gasped.

'This is SO not fair,' Lauren said, her face pale with anger. 'It's looking like it really *was* Max who stole the watch, but now the police suspect the hotel staff, and everyone feels really down about it.'

Mia patted Lauren's arm comfortingly. She knew how much her friend loved the hotel and how upset she was about this.

'We *still* don't have any real proof though,' Becky pointed out.

'You're right, Becks,' Jas agreed reluctantly. 'We need to get proof somehow.'

'If Max is planning to sell the watch on that antiques website, he must have some emails or documents about it on his laptop,' Mia said thoughtfully. 'We need to have a closer look at his computer . . .'

The girls all thought for a moment. Then Jas's eyes lit up.

'I've got a plan for that!' she said. 'We wait until Max has gone out tomorrow – without his laptop, obviously – and then we shoot up to his room while the maids are cleaning his floor. Mia and I will sneak in and then Mia can look at Max's laptop, while I search his room for the watch. Simple!'

CHAPTER FIVE

The girls stared at each other in excitement.

'Do you really think we can pull it off?' Mia asked.

'Course we can!' Jas said confidently.

'It sounds good to me,' Lauren agreed. 'I'll help you search Max's room, Jas, and Becky can be the look-out—'

But Becky was shaking her head.

'No, Lauren, it's too risky,' she said firmly. 'You need to be completely out of the way because if something goes wrong and we get caught, you'll be in *huge* trouble with your parents.'

Lauren felt really disappointed, but she knew in her heart of hearts that Becky was right. 'OK,' she sighed. 'Thanks for thinking about me, Becks.'

'You can be another look-out, like me,' Becky offered. 'Now' – she glanced around at the other

three, who were wide-eyed with nervous anticipation – 'let's decide *exactly* how we're going to
do this. It's really serious stuff, and we can't
afford to put a foot wrong.'

'If we get it *right*, hopefully we can find out
the truth about Max once and for all,' Lauren said
solemnly.

'I'm so nervous, I can't sit still,' Lauren whispered
to Becky, Mia and Jas.

It was the following day after school and the
girls were perched on one of the huge, squashy
leather sofas in reception, watching and waiting
and *hoping* that Max would leave the hotel and
go out for the evening. They were fairly sure he
hadn't gone out yet because Emma, one of the
receptionists, had told them that she'd seen Max
come in from a business appointment less than
half an hour ago.

Fridays were usually quite busy with new
guests checking in for the weekend, and there
were lots of people milling around in reception.
Lauren fixed her eyes on the lifts, praying that
they wouldn't miss Max coming out and leaving
the hotel among the crowds.

'What's that funny gurgling noise?' Becky
asked, raising her eyebrows.

'It's my tummy,' Jas explained apologetically. 'I was so nervous, I hardly ate any lunch!'

Suddenly Lauren gave a loud groan. She hadn't seen Max, but she *had* spotted Charlie. Her brother had just come into reception and he was marching around, studying all the guests curiously. A moment later he saw the girls and zoomed towards them, a suspicious look on his face.

'Here comes Charlie,' Lauren said quickly. 'Act normally!'

'That'll be hard for you, Jas,' Mia said with a grin.

'Cheek!' Jas retorted, smiling too.

Charlie stopped in front of the sofa and eyeballed the girls. Lauren tried to look as wide-eyed and innocent as possible.

'You're up to something!' Charlie accused them immediately. 'You *never* hang out here usually. What are you doing?'

'Nothing,' the girls said together.

Charlie frowned. 'I don't believe you,' he said, folding his arms. 'And I'm not moving until you tell me what's going on!'

Charlie was now blocking the girls' view of the lifts, and Lauren was really worried that Max would come out and they'd miss him. Then, to her relief, she saw Mrs Lloyd emerge from the café-bar.

'Look, there's Mrs Lloyd,' she said, pointing the elderly woman out to Charlie. 'I suppose you've questioned her already about the theft of her watch?'

'Er – no,' Charlie said a little sheepishly.

'Not much of a spy, are you, then?' Lauren said with a sniff. 'I thought you and Joe were on a secret mission to find out who'd stolen it.'

'Don't worry, we will,' Charlie replied. 'And I'm going to find out what you lot are up to as well – my name isn't Bond for nothing!' Then he shot off after Mrs Lloyd, who was heading towards the hotel lounge.

'Great stuff, Lauren!' Mia said. 'I thought we were never going to get rid of him.'

'And not a moment too soon,' Jas chimed in. 'Look, here comes Max.'

Lauren's heart skipped an excited beat as she saw Max step out of the lift and hurry through reception. He was wearing an expensive-looking dark-grey suit and he had his briefcase with him.

'He doesn't have his laptop bag,' Becky pointed out. 'Which means the laptop should still be in his room.'

'Let's go,' Jas said. 'Lauren, you know what you have to do, don't you?'

Lauren nodded. 'I stay here while you three head up to the ninth floor,' she replied. 'And if Max comes back, I phone Becky, who'll be hanging around in the corridor.'

'And then I'll knock three times on Max's door to give you time to get out,' Becky went on, glancing at Jas and Mia. 'Here goes!'

'Good luck,' Lauren said as her three friends hurried over to the lifts. She wished she was going with them, but it was important that someone stayed downstairs to watch for Max returning unexpectedly. Lauren felt hot and cold all over at the thought of Max discovering Jas and Mia sneaking around his room. It was up to her to make sure that didn't happen . . .

'The maids have already started the turndown service in the rooms,' Becky whispered as she, Mia and Jas came out of the lifts onto the ninth floor. They'd been counting on the fact that every evening the maids made the beds ready for the night and left a chocolate on each guest's pillow.

The girls could see trolleys piled with fresh towels and chocolates stationed along the corridor and some of the bedroom doors stood open, including Max's.

'It looks like someone is working in Max's room at the moment,' Mia said in a low voice. 'Jas, we'd better keep out of sight.'

Max's room was at the end of the corridor, so Jas and Mia slipped round the corner and waited there in silence. Meanwhile, Becky remained loitering outside Max's door. After a few moments, Jas and Mia heard footsteps. Jas peered cautiously round the corner and saw Rachel, the chambermaid, coming out of Max's room, carrying a pile of dirty towels.

'Oh, hi, Becky,' she said, looking surprised. 'What are you doing here?'

'I'm looking for Lauren,' Becky explained. 'Charlie said she was up here.'

Rachel shook her head. 'I think he was having you on!' she said with a smile. 'That boy's always up to something.'

Putting her finger to her lips, Jas beckoned to Mia. This was part of their plan. While Becky was distracting Rachel, Jas and Mia would creep into Max's room through the open door.

'Charlie says he's going to try and find out who stole Mrs Lloyd's watch,' Becky said to Rachel. She tried not to glance beyond the chambermaid at Jas and Mia who were now sidling round the corner towards the door.

Rachel frowned. 'Well, I hope *someone* does,' she replied. 'It's not very nice, all of us being under suspicion.'

As Rachel made to turn back towards the room, Becky quickly clutched her arm.

'Look!' Becky gasped, trying to distract the maid so that she didn't spot Mia and Jas. 'What's that?' And she pointed down the corridor at a large pot plant.

Rachel turned and glanced at it as Mia and Jas inched their way towards the open door. 'You mean the plant?' She raised her eyebrows. 'What about it?'

'Er – I *thought* I saw Charlie hiding behind it,' Becky gabbled, saying the first thing that came into her head. 'And I think he had a water pistol in his hand!'

Rachel took a few steps down the corridor and peered at the plant. Hoping that her empty tummy wouldn't rumble and give her away, Jas rushed silently into Max's room behind Rachel's back. Mia followed her, and the two of them hid behind the open door. They both breathed sighs of relief when they heard Rachel say, 'You must have been imagining it, Becky – there's no one

there! Well, I'd better get on. See you later.'
Then, to Jas and Mia's relief, Rachel swung the
door shut without looking into the room again.

'We did it!' Jas gasped, feeling triumphant
that her plan had worked. 'I wish my knees
would stop wobbling like two jellies, though!'

'We'd better hurry,' Mia said urgently. 'Look,
there's Max's laptop on the desk. You search for
the watch, Jas.'

'Where should I start?' Jas wondered aloud,
staring around the large room. 'There are loads of
hiding-places.'

'Try the room safe in the wardrobe,' Mia
suggested as she opened the laptop. 'The watch
is valuable so Max would probably keep it in the
safe, wouldn't he?'

'I hope not,' Jas groaned, 'because if the safe's
locked, we won't be able to find out if the watch
is in there or not.'

As Mia sat down at the desk in front of the
laptop and turned it on, Jas ran over to the
wardrobe. She threw back the doors and
immediately spotted the safe sitting on the floor
of the cupboard. To Jas's relief, the door of the
safe was open.

'The safe's empty,' she called to Mia, who
was now tapping away on the keyboard. 'That

means Max has either got the watch with him, or it's hidden somewhere in this room.'

'*If* he stole it,' Mia reminded her.

'I'm sure Max is the thief,' Jas replied confidently. 'And if that watch is here, I'm going to find it!'

For the next twenty minutes, Jas searched the room carefully while Mia concentrated on Max's laptop. First Jas searched the cupboards and drawers and all the obvious hiding-places. Her heart started to pound with excitement when she caught a glint of gold in one of the drawers, but she was very disappointed when it turned out to be a pair of gold cufflinks. Jas got down on her hands and knees and looked under the bed, checking underneath the duvet and the pillows too. She searched the adjoining bathroom thoroughly, even though there wasn't really much room to hide anything in there. She even peeped inside a huge vase of dried flowers and grasses that stood on the window ledge. But there was no sign of an antique gold watch.

'I hope you're having better luck than me, Mia,' Jas sighed, at last. 'I haven't found a single thing!'

'No, I'm not, actually.' Mia pulled a face. 'I managed to log on easily enough, and I've checked the Internet history, the cookies and Max's documents. I've even decoded his password and checked his emails, and I can't find *anything* about antique watches or buying and selling antiques!' She frowned at Jas. 'I'm beginning to think Max is innocent, you know.'

'But he's so *smarmy*,' Jas pointed out. 'OK, OK, I know that's not a crime!'

'I think we'd better get out of here,' said Mia. 'I'll just close the laptop down.'

But before Mia could do so, their attention was caught by the sound of Becky's voice outside in the corridor.

'Oh, hi, MAX! How ARE you? And how's ISABELLA?'

Jas and Mia looked at each other in complete panic.

'Becky's talking to Max!' Mia gasped. 'He must be right outside the door!'

'And Becky's trying to warn us by speaking loudly,' Jas whispered anxiously. 'Why didn't she knock on the door like we agreed? We'd better hide, Mia – and fast!'

CHAPTER SIX

Mia was so nervous, she was shaking all over. She didn't have time to shut the computer down properly so instead she quickly closed the lid, sending it into sleep mode.

By this time the girls could hear Max inserting his room card into the door lock. Mia was almost paralysed with fright. But then Jas, her face pale, grabbed Mia's arm and pulled her across the room towards the bed. Both girls hit the floor and rolled silently into the gap between the bed and the floor, Mia clutching her bag with Dillon inside. Then, just a few seconds later, they heard the door swing open.

Max walked into the room and bent down to put his briefcase on the rug near the desk. Mia could see him clearly from where she was hiding. She'd never been so scared in all her life as she lay rigid under the bed next to Jas. The power light on the computer was flashing, indicating that it was in sleep mode, and Mia prayed desperately that Max wouldn't notice. If he did, he'd realize that someone had switched the computer on in his absence . . .

Max was now walking over to the bed. Mia held her breath, sure that they were about to be discovered. Her heart was thumping so loudly, she was surprised Max couldn't hear it. Mia didn't even dare glance at Jas as Max stopped just a few centimetres away from them.

Suddenly there was a tap at the door and Max strode across the room to open it.

'Hi, Suzanne,' he said. 'Come in.'

Jas cast a look of dismay at Mia, who knew exactly what her friend was thinking. If Max had a visitor – Suzanne – he wasn't likely to go out again in a hurry, was he? How long would they be stuck here under the bed? Mia fretted. Becky and Lauren would be going frantic. And now Dillon had started running about inside her bag! He loved being carried around and was usually very quiet and relaxed, but the sound of Max's voice always seemed to upset him. Mia hoped Dillon didn't scrabble around too much and make a noise.

'I've been trying to get hold of you for ages, Max,' Suzanne grumbled as she walked into the room. Mia couldn't see anything of her except long legs in black denim and a pair of sparkly pink ballet pumps.

'Sorry, I had a bit of business to sort out,' Max said smoothly. Just then Mia heard a muffled ringing sound. After a second or two, she realized it was coming from inside Max's brief-case. Mia bit her lip, petrified that Max might notice them under the bed as he bent down to pick up his case. 'Excuse me.'

Mia breathed a silent sigh of relief as Max grabbed his briefcase and lifted it up without spotting them. But when he laid the briefcase flat on the desk and punched in the code to open it, she began to panic again. Max was *sure* to notice the computer light this time – it was right there next to him! Mia didn't dare turn to look at Jas, who must have been as nervous as she was. But luckily Max was intent on getting his phone out in time to answer the call. Mia could hardly believe their luck had held. But for how much longer?

'Hello? Yes, it's me. Where are you? OK, let's do that.'

Meanwhile Suzanne wandered over to the bed and sat down on it. It creaked a little and Jas threw Mia a look of horror. She looked even more scared a moment later when Suzanne kicked off her ballet pumps under the bed, and one landed very close to Jas's nose.

'Right, I'm going down to the bar for a business meeting,' Max said to Suzanne when he'd finished his call. 'Do you want to come?'

Under the bed Mia and Jas exchanged relieved smiles. This would be their chance to escape!

Suzanne yawned loudly. 'No, I think I'll stay and have a shower,' she replied. 'See you later.'

Mia almost groaned with frustration but managed to stop herself. The girls heard Max leave the room, shutting the door behind him, and then they heard Suzanne pad into the bathroom on bare feet.

'What are we going to do, Jas?' Mia whispered urgently.

'We'll have to try and make a dash for it while she's in the shower,' Jas whispered back. 'The sound of the water running will mask any noise we make—'

'Ssh!' Mia hissed. 'She's coming back!'

Suzanne had undressed in the bathroom and was now wearing one of the hotel's fluffy white robes. Mia could see her bare legs and the hem of the robe. She threw her clothes on the bed, then leaned forward to wrap her head in a towel, and Mia caught a glimpse of long blonde hair.

'Get ready to go for it as soon as she turns the water on,' Jas murmured in Mia's ear as Suzanne walked over to the sound system and began fiddling with the radio.

Mia nodded. But then she saw something moving out of the corner of her eye. Mia turned her head slightly and, to her horror, saw Dillon the gerbil scurry past her ear.

Jas saw him too, and her eyes almost popped out of her head. Before the girls could stop him, Dillon scampered out from under the bed and ran across the carpet.

'EEEK!' Suzanne screamed. 'There's a mouse in here! Help!' She threw off the robe, jumped into her clothes and shoes as fast as she could and fled out of the room. Mia and Jas could hear her running off down the corridor.

Immediately the two girls scrambled out from under the bed.

'Clever little Dillon!' Jas gasped. 'He's given us a chance to escape. Did you let him out on purpose, Mia?'

Mia shook her head. 'Look, the zip on my bag has come open a bit,' she said, showing Jas the bag. 'Dillon must have squeezed out.'

'We'd better find him before Suzanne comes

back with an army of housekeeping staff and a mousetrap!' Jas said urgently, looking around.

Mia turned white with fear at the thought. 'Where *is* he?'

'There he goes!' Jas said as she spotted Dillon's long tail disappearing into the bathroom.

Mia and Jas chased after him, but the gerbil was nowhere to be seen when they ran in.

'He's in here *somewhere*,' Jas panted, peering around.

'Dillon!' Mia cried as she saw him pop out from behind the base of the wash-basin. 'Come here!'

But Dillon raced off out of the bathroom and back into the bedroom. As he scuttled across the carpet, Jas made a grab for him and missed, almost tumbling over as she did so.

'Dillon looks like he's having a great time!' Jas wailed in frustration. 'I don't think he's ill any more, Mia – he seems to have made a full recovery!'

Now Dillon was heading straight for Max's briefcase, which was still lying on the floor. The briefcase was wedged open a little by a wad of paperwork sticking out, and Dillon wriggled inside it through the gap.

'Got you!' Jas said triumphantly. 'I'll open the briefcase, Mia, and you grab Dillon.'

Mia nodded, and Jas eased the lid of the briefcase up carefully so she didn't frighten Dillon. He was sitting there blinking up at them, and Mia and Jas both gasped in astonishment.

Because Dillon was perched on top of a gold necklace shaped like a collar, and in the very centre of the necklace was an enormous ruby that glittered and sparkled with dazzling scarlet fire.

CHAPTER SEVEN

Mia and Jas stared, speechless, at the incredible ruby.

'It's the legendary necklace that Isabella's going to wear at the Kaspari jewellery launch!' Mia said in hushed tones as she scooped Dillon up and popped him safely back in her bag. 'The one we're doing our project about.'

'It *can't* be,' Jas pointed out with a frown. 'It's really valuable – Max wouldn't be carrying it around in his briefcase with him, if it was real! Oh!' Her eyes widened. 'Maybe he's stolen it, like we thought he'd stolen Mrs Lloyd's watch!'

But Mia shook her head. 'If the necklace had been stolen, it'd be all over the news by now,' she said. 'No, I think this one must be a copy. Maybe Isabella's been using it for some photo-shoots or something.'

'Or maybe Kaspari have given her a copy of the necklace as a gift,' Jazz guessed. 'Anyway, we don't have time for this now. Let's get out of here!'

'I'll just close down Max's computer properly.' Mia ran over to the desk. 'Then he'll never know it's been touched.' Quickly she turned the computer off. Then she and Jas hurried noise-lessly over to the door. They slipped out into the corridor and bumped straight into Charlie.

'Oh!' Jas exclaimed, flustered. 'You gave me a fright!'

'What are you doing hanging around here, anyway, Charlie?' asked Mia.

But Charlie didn't say a word. He stared at the two girls with wide, horrified eyes, and then shot off down the corridor.

'What's bugging *him*?' Jas wanted to know.

Just then Becky appeared from round the corner, walking as fast as she could without actually running. 'Oh, I'm *sooo* sorry, you two!' she groaned, looking absolutely mortified.

'What happened, Becks?' Jas asked. 'You were supposed to let us know that Max was on his way.'

Becky pulled a face. 'I was just lurking around minding my own business when The Snoop turned up!' she wailed. 'She stood there and gave me a lecture about how we girls aren't guests at the hotel and so we shouldn't be hanging around the corridors like the Mayfair Park is some kind of youth centre!'

'Trust The Snoop to spoil all our plans,' sighed Mia sympathetically. She could see that poor Becky was looking really upset at having let them down.

'Anyway, I could hear my phone buzzing away in my pocket and I guessed it was Lauren warning me that Max was coming,' Becky went on ruefully, 'but I couldn't check my phone or knock on Max's door, not while The Snoop was still lecturing me. So I was just really polite and nodded and smiled and hoped she'd go away, and at last she did! But by then it was too late because Max was coming out of the lift!'

'Well, at least you managed to warn us by talking loudly,' Jas said, giving Becky a comforting squeeze. 'Mia and I just managed to hide before Max saw us.'

'So what happened then?' Becky asked eagerly. 'Did you find the watch?'

Mia shook her head. 'No, we didn't, but let's go and catch up with Lauren first, and then we'll tell you the whole story,' she replied. 'You know,' Mia went on as they headed for the lifts, 'it's a shame the Mayfair Park *isn't* a youth centre

– then wrinkly old prunes like The Snoop wouldn't be allowed in!'

Becky laughed, looking a lot brighter, which
Mia was glad to see. As they got into the lift,
they saw Mrs Stoop come out of another
lift opposite them. She looked furious.

'Mice!' Mrs Stoop was muttering to herself as
she hurried off towards Max's room. 'Mice in my
hotel – I've never heard of such a thing!'

Jas and Mia glanced at each other and burst
into fits of laughter as the lift doors slid shut.

'What's going on?' Becky asked, bewildered.

'Well, Mia and I couldn't have escaped without Dillon's help,' Jas chuckled. 'We've got a
really exciting tale to tell you and Lauren!'

The girls had already arranged to meet up
with Lauren in the Bonds' flat after the search of
Max's room. But when they arrived, Mia was
surprised to see Charlie waiting for them along
with Lauren.

'Hey, guys,' Lauren said eagerly. 'Did the plan
work? Did you find anything?'

'Er – no to both,' Mia replied cautiously,
glancing at Charlie. Lauren grinned at her.

'Don't worry about Charlie,' she explained.
'He knows the whole story. I had to tell him
because when he bumped into you and Jas

running out of Max's room, he thought *you two* were the watch thieves!'

'What!' Jas exclaimed. Charlie, meanwhile, was looking a little sheepish.

'Well, you *did* look really suspicious,' he muttered.

'Luckily, Charlie came to tell me first,' Lauren went on, her eyes twinkling. 'He wanted me to help him put you under citizen's arrest!'

'Good work, Charlie,' Mia said kindly. 'You'll make a great secret agent one day!'

'So, is Max the thief or not?' Charlie asked.

'And how come the plan didn't work?' Lauren wanted to know.

'Let's get a drink and sit down,' Jas suggested with a grin. 'It's a long story . . .'

'I just can't believe The Snoop was sticking her nose in like that!' Lauren said indignantly. She was floating on her back in the warm waters of the hotel swimming pool while the other girls swam lazily around her. It was early evening and the pool was empty except for the girls and Charlie and Joe. Usually the girls loved having the pool to themselves, but Charlie and Joe were being particularly annoying and dive-bombing them every few minutes. 'She really messed up our whole plan,' Lauren went on. 'What if Jas and Mia hadn't managed to hide before Max came in? We'd be in *dead* trouble now.'

'If it wasn't for Dillon, Mia and I might still be under that bed!' Jas said as she bobbed along in the water next to Lauren. 'It was lucky Suzanne, whoever she is, is scared of mice.'

'So who *is* Suzanne, d'you think?' asked Becky.

'Maybe she's Max's girlfriend,' Jas guessed. 'I wonder if—' Then she gave a loud scream as Charlie and Joe leaped off the side of the pool and landed in the water right next to her with a huge splash. 'Stop it, you two!'

Charlie and Joe surfaced, spluttering with laughter. They whispered something to each other, and then they both dived down and grabbed Lauren's legs, trying to pull her underwater.

'Let go of me, you little pests!' Lauren yelled. Jas, Mia and Becky rushed to her rescue, but the two boys had already swum off, chortling loudly. Rolling her eyes, Lauren chucked an inflatable rubber ring after them, but missed.

'I wish some of the guests would come for a swim,' Becky grumbled, 'then those two would have to behave themselves. I need to relax a bit.

My ordeal with The Snoop has left me exhausted!'

'So I guess we were wrong about Max, then, girls.' Mia began floating alongside Lauren. 'I wonder what *did* happen to Mrs Lloyd's watch, though?'

'It's a shame you didn't find it, but I'm glad Max wasn't the thief,' Becky mused. 'It would have been awful for Isabella.'

At that moment the automatic glass doors slid open and Isabella walked in. She was wearing a white towelling robe and her long dark hair was knotted on top of her head. Charlie and Joe, who were messing around with rubber rings at the other side of the pool, immediately quietened down and began swimming lengths with innocent looks on their faces.

'Well, at least Isabella's stopped Charlie and Joe from being complete pains!' Becky murmured. 'Do you think we should say hello?'

Jas shook her head. 'I don't think we'd better disturb her,' she replied. 'Not after the way she spoke to us last time!'

'Hello, girls,' Isabella called. She had stopped by the poolside and was waving at them. The girls exchanged surprised glances as they waved back.

'Hi, Isabella,' Becky called a little warily.

'I'm just off to the spa to have my nails painted for the launch tomorrow,' Isabella explained with a dazzling smile. 'I was wondering whether to stick with the ruby-red theme, or whether to go for something contrasting like a pearly pink varnish. What do you think?'

'Ruby-red, definitely,' said Jas.

'Do you think so?' Isabella laughed. 'Yes, you're right! By the way, can you come to the spa in about half an hour? My nails will be almost done by then, and I have a surprise for you.' And she walked off.

The girls stared at each other in shock.

'*Well!*' Lauren shrugged her shoulders in disbelief. 'Looks like Isabella is all sweetness and light again today. How weird!'

'Do you think she meant what she said about a surprise for us?' Becky speculated eagerly.

'Who knows?' Jas said, rolling her eyes. 'She might change her mind again in the next five minutes!'

'Maybe we'd better wait and see and not get our hopes up,' Mia suggested.

'Too late!' Becky sighed, pulling a comical face. She was absolutely *dying* to know what Isabella had meant.

'Five–four–three–two–one!' Charlie shouted as he and Joe prepared to launch themselves off the side of the pool in the girls' direction again. This time the girls swam away quickly as the boys crashed into the water.

'Right, you two, we're getting out now,' Lauren called as she floated over to the steps. 'And that means *you* have to, as well. You know Mum and Dad's rules.'

Charlie pulled a cross-eyed face at her. 'You lot are so boring!' he grumbled. 'Come on, Joe. We ought to get on with our secret mission to find Mrs Lloyd's watch, anyway!'

They all climbed out of the pool and went to get changed. As Becky dried her blonde curls with the hairdryer, she silently hoped that Isabella would be nice to them and not go into diva mode. It would be *so* disappointing . . .

'Oh, there you are, girls!' Isabella nodded and smiled at Becky, Lauren, Jas and Mia as they went into the spa, looking rather hesitant and cautious. One of the manicurists, Elena, was just adding a final coat of clear gloss to Isabella's deep-red nails. 'What do you think?' Isabella went on, holding out her hands to show the colour off.

'It's fab!' Becky breathed, secretly relieved

that Isabella was still in a good mood. 'It'll go beautifully with your dress and the ruby shoes.'

'What time is the launch tomorrow, Isabella?' Mia asked. 'We'd really like to see you in your outfit when you leave the hotel.'

Isabella laughed. 'Oh, I think we can do better than that!' she said. 'Becky, there's something for all of you on the table there.'

Becky went over to the table. There lay four large, square pieces of cream-coloured card covered with gold writing and edged with a glittering ruby border. Becky let out a gasp.

'Oh! Invitations to the Kaspari launch tomorrow!'

Becky, Mia, Jas and Lauren stared at each other in delighted disbelief.

Isabella nodded. 'Yes, I do hope you'll come.'

'Are you kidding?' Jas exclaimed. 'Of course we'll come!' Then she blushed, turning as red as Isabella's nail varnish.

'Good, that's what I hoped you'd say!' With a smile, Isabella stood up. 'You'll be able to see the new collection, as well as watch the photo-shoot of me wearing the famous gold and ruby necklace. I'm going to be mingling with the crowd too, and chatting with the guests, so I'll catch up with you again then.' She turned to the manicurist. 'Thank you so much for my manicure, Elena. I'll see you at the launch tomorrow, girls.'

'Thanks, Isabella,' Becky said, hardly able to believe her luck.

'Yes, thank you,' Jas, Mia and Lauren added together.

'This is just the best thing!' Becky squealed when Isabella had left. She threw her arms around Mia, Jas and Lauren and the four of them jumped up and down in excitement. 'I can't wait!'

'I'll tell you what,' said Elena, smiling as she watched their celebrations. 'I have a bit of free time now. Why don't I give you all a manicure for tomorrow so you look your best?'

'Would you, Elena?' Becky said eagerly. 'That would be *excellent*.'

'And that means you too, Lauren!' Jas ordered as Becky sat down opposite Elena and held out her hands. 'We've all got to dress up and look fabulous so we don't let Isabella down.'

'OK,' Lauren agreed with a grin. 'I guess this is a special occasion.'

Elena filed and painted Becky's nails, and then started on Mia's. A few moments later the doors into the spa opened and, to the girls' amazement,

Charlie and Joe came rushing in, their faces red with suppressed excitement.

'Have you come for a facial, guys?' Lauren asked solemnly, shooting a secret grin at the others. 'Or maybe a manicure?'

'I *told* you we'd find it!' Charlie burst out, glowing with pride.

'Find what?' Becky asked.

'Mrs Lloyd's watch!' Charlie and Joe shouted together. Then, whooping loudly, they gave each other a high five.

'You're joking!' Jas exclaimed.

'Do we look like we're joking?' Charlie asked indignantly. 'Mrs Lloyd said we were the cleverest boys she'd ever met!'

'OK, so tell all!' Mia said as Elena began to paint her nails pale pink. 'Where did you find it?'

'Well, when we left the pool,' Charlie began, 'Joe and I tracked Mrs Lloyd down to the café-bar, just like secret agents do.'

'So you spotted Mrs Lloyd in the café-bar,' Lauren commented. 'Then what?'

'We interrogated her,' Joe said solemnly.

'Really?' Becky said, trying not to laugh. 'I hope you were nice to her.'

'*Course* we were,' Joe agreed. 'She even bought us lemonade!'

'So you asked Mrs Lloyd where she last remembered seeing her watch?' Jas said.

Charlie nodded. 'We wanted to know about her movements yesterday to identify a possible location for the missing item,' he explained.

Lauren had to bite the inside of her cheek to stop herself from smiling. 'You mean you were trying to find out if there was somewhere she hadn't looked for the watch!' she interpreted.

'That was our plan,' Charlie confirmed. 'And it worked! We discovered that our client—'

'Mrs Lloyd, you mean,' Mia supplied.

'Yes, her!' Charlie said impatiently. 'We discovered that she'd got a bag of laundry ready to send down to housekeeping, and—'

'The watch had fallen in the laundry bag!' Joe burst out.

'I wanted to say that bit, Joe!' Charlie complained.

'Well, it *was* me who found it in the laundry bag,' Joe pointed out a touch smugly.

'But it was me who suggested looking there!' Charlie retorted.

Becky glanced at the other girls and raised her eyebrows as Charlie and Joe continued to chatter excitedly. Here was proof, but not the proof they'd been looking for. Max Carroll definitely wasn't the watch thief after all.

'Well, no wonder we couldn't find the watch or any mention of it on Max's laptop,' Mia remarked as they left the spa an hour or so later. 'He never had it to begin with!'

'I'm so glad Mrs Lloyd has got it back now,' Lauren said. 'It was horrible when everyone in the hotel was under suspicion.'

'I'm glad too, but I'm also just a *teensy* bit disappointed,' Jas admitted, admiring her pearly-pink nails. 'It was really fun having a mystery to investigate, and now it turns out it wasn't really a mystery at all!'

'Charlie's going to be totally unbearable from now on.' Lauren groaned. 'He was sure he was going to solve the mystery of the stolen watch – and now he has!'

'Well, at least we've got something to look forward to,' Becky pointed out. 'It's the big launch of the Kaspari jewellery collection tomorrow – and we've got tickets!'

CHAPTER EIGHT

'Have a great time, girls,' Mrs Bond called as Becky, Mia, Jas and Lauren climbed carefully out of the car. They were all wearing their very best outfits, and even though the Columbine Gallery was only a few minutes' walk from the hotel, Lauren's mum had offered them a lift.

'So that you don't ruin all your finery!' she had said with a grin. The traffic had been very busy, though, because of the launch, so they'd crawled slowly all the way to the gallery, while the girls fizzed with impatience. They'd met up a few hours previously in Lauren's room to get ready, and there had been a lot of excitement when Elena and a couple of the other beauticians from the spa had offered to help with their hair and make-up.

Now Becky was so thrilled, she could hardly breathe as she stared up at the imposing stone-built gallery. A huge poster of Isabella's familiar face was hanging on the outside of the building, and underneath in gold and red letters was written: *Isabella Duval – the face of the new Kaspari Ruby Collection. Launching here today!*

'Look at all the people waiting to see Isabella!' Jas gasped, smoothing down her crimson silk shift mini-dress. The girls had all decided to wear something red in honour of the occasion. 'There are *hundreds* of them.'

The entrance to the gallery was up a long flight of stone steps, laid with a ruby-red carpet. There were steel barriers at the bottom of the steps that were manned by security guards who were carefully checking everyone's tickets. Behind the barriers on one side of the steps were TV crews and paparazzi photographers, cameras and flashguns at the ready. Opposite them, also behind barriers, were crowds of people hoping for a quick glimpse of Isabella on her way into the gallery. There were police around to keep an eye on them and make sure things didn't get out of hand.

'This is so exciting!' Lauren beamed. She was wearing skinny black trousers, a wide, stretchy black belt with a silver clasp and a red sparkly T-shirt that Jas had lent her. 'I guess we get to go and stand up there with all the other posh people who have tickets!' And she pointed at the top of the stairs. The huge glass doors of the gallery stood open, and men wearing dinner jackets and women in stunning designer dresses were gathered at the top of the steps, waiting for Isabella to arrive.

Feeling like a film star herself in her cream sequinned mini-dress and glittery red tights, Becky led the way over to the heavily guarded entrance.

'Look at the other guests!' Jas breathed as they joined the queue of ticket-holders. 'That's the girl who nearly won *The X Factor* just in front of us!'

'And there's Marc Alexander!' Lauren's eyes were almost popping out as she stared at the good-looking young actor in his dinner jacket. 'He was in Isabella's last film, wasn't he?'

'Tickets, please,' one of the burly security men said.

The girls handed their tickets over. The guard inspected them closely and then stepped aside to let them through.

'I hope I don't trip up in these wedge heels and make a fool of myself in front of all these people,' Lauren murmured as they walked up the steps.

'Me too,' Mia agreed. Becky thought she looked *gorgeous* in her midnight-blue dress embroidered with silver stars and her long dark hair piled up on top of her head. 'That would be beyond embarrassing!'

'*Please* tell me Dillon isn't in there,' Jas said, pointing at Mia's tiny red evening bag.

'No, he isn't,' Mia replied. 'I left him at home. He's obviously feeling better after giving us the run-around in Max's room yesterday, but I thought the excitement of this might be too much for him.'

As they reached the top of the steps and joined the rest of the guests, the girls heard the sound of a car purring its way up to the gallery. Then they saw a deep-red, shiny limo draw to a halt at the foot of the steps, and the crowd burst into cheers and applause.

'Here she is!' Jas said.

The noise of the crowd was deafening as Max jumped out of the car and then opened the door for Isabella. The crowd went wild as she climbed out, looking stunning in the ruby-red gown, and waved at them, smiling graciously. Immediately the photographers began snapping pictures as Isabella went over to sign some autographs for the crowd.

'Oh, Isabella looks so beautiful!' Jas exclaimed, grabbing her phone from her bag and taking a quick photo. Becky and Lauren did the same. Mia had brought a camera with her to take photos for their project so she began clicking away too.

Isabella seemed rather edgy and nervous as she signed autographs, Becky noticed. And Max was looking a little uneasy and impatient too. He soon tried to get Isabella away from the crowd, taking her arm and escorting her up the steps as she held up her long skirt so she didn't trip on it.

As she watched, Becky noticed something rather puzzling.

'Look at Isabella's feet,' she whispered to Jas, Mia and Lauren. 'She isn't wearing the ruby shoes after all!'

The others gazed at Isabella and saw that she was wearing a pair of flat red shoes under her gown instead of the sparkling high heels she'd shown them a few days ago.

'Maybe Isabella changed her mind because the heels were so high and she was worried about tripping on these steps,' Lauren suggested. 'I know I was!'

'And she's going to be at the launch for ages

doing photos and interviews,' Jas added. 'She probably thought flats would be more comfy.'

But Becky wasn't convinced. 'Isabella said she didn't mind wearing high heels all the time,' she pointed out. 'So why has she changed her mind?'

'Maybe she broke one of the heels and had to wear another pair of shoes instead,' Mia said.

Becky nodded. That seemed like the most obvious explanation.

Isabella and Max were now at the top of the steps, where they paused and turned so that the press photographers could get more pictures. As Isabella did so, she caught Becky's eye. Becky gave her a tiny wave, but she was a bit mortified when Isabella didn't even smile back at her. She just seemed to stare right through the girls as if she didn't even know them. She was clearly back in diva mode. Becky felt disappointed all over again.

'I just waved at Isabella, but she acted like she'd never seen me before,' Becky whispered to her friends. Isabella and Max were now entering the gallery, and the guests were following them inside.

'I suppose she must feel pretty overwhelmed by all these people,' Mia said.

'Or maybe she's just in one of her bad moods again!' Jas suggested with a shrug. 'Anyway, we're *really* lucky to be invited so let's just enjoy it and go look at the collection. We'll have a great time.'

Becky nodded, but she still felt a little puzzled by Isabella's behaviour. Superstars really were *very* difficult people to get along with, Becky thought as she, Jas, Mia and Lauren went into the gallery . . .

'. . . and it is my great pleasure and privilege, as the managing director of Kaspari, to welcome you to this launch of our magnificent new collection.' Antonio Kaspari, a tall middle-aged man wearing an elegant dove-grey suit, was opening the jewellery launch with a speech to all the guests. 'And as you already know, the highlight of the event will be a photo-shoot with the new face of Kaspari, the dazzling Isabella Duval, wearing the legendary Cleopatra necklace . . .'

Becky glanced over at Isabella, who was standing on the other side of the room with Max and some other members of the Kaspari family. Isabella still looked a little nervous, but that was understandable, Becky thought. After all, this was an extremely important occasion. Isabella was the guest of honour, but there were lots of other famous faces around too, and the girls hadn't been able to resist celeb-spotting while Mr Kaspari was making his speech.

'There are so many famous people here!' Becky gasped as a couple of England footballers passed by with glamorous girlfriends in tow. Becky had never seen so many gorgeous dresses under one roof before. The guests were a select mix of journalists, celebrities and wealthy customers who could afford to buy the very expensive Kaspari jewellery. 'Everywhere I look, I see someone else I recognize.'

'They're probably wondering who on earth *we* are!' Jas pointed out and the others giggled.

When Mr Kaspari finished speaking and was warmly applauded, the guests began to move around the room, mingling and chatting. But the girls stayed in a corner, just taking in the spectacular sights all around them. The gallery had been decorated with a ruby theme – there were swags of red and white roses around the windows and huge plush red velvet sofas for guests to perch on. Even the waiters who were serving the guests with pink champagne and canapés were wearing red dinner jackets. The new Kaspari collection was displayed in glass cabinets around the room, the rubies, diamonds and gold shimmering and glittering in the lights. Becky was longing to have a closer look at the jewellery, but so many of the other guests were now clustered around the cabinets, it was impossible for the girls to see anything at the moment. The biggest crowd was at the far end of the room. Lots of people had gathered around another glass case that was guarded by four uniformed security men with walkie-talkies.

'That must be Cleopatra's famous gold and ruby necklace that inspired the collection,' Mia said. 'I'm dying to see it and take some photos for our project.'

'I'm thirsty,' Lauren murmured as a waiter whisked past them carrying a tray of pink champagne. 'I don't suppose they'll let us have any champagne, though!'

As if by magic, another waiter appeared at Lauren's elbow. He was holding a tray with four tall glasses filled with ruby-coloured liquid and topped with paper and diamanté parasols.

'Fruit cocktail, miss?' he enquired.

Eagerly each of the girls took one of the glasses.

'Yum!' Jas said, sipping the ruby-red liquid. 'I can taste strawberries and raspberries and vanilla.'

At that moment there was a drum roll, followed by a burst of sweet, haunting Egyptian music. The doors were flung back, and a troupe of acrobats, dressed in Egyptian tunics, back-flipped into the room. They were followed by barefoot dancers wearing long, gauzy, glittery skirts and tops and gold bracelets and anklets. The dancers began to sway around, weaving their way between the guests as the acrobats tumbled from one end of the room to the other. There were gasps of appreciation from the crowd.

'This is so cool!' Jas exclaimed, her eyes almost popping out of her head at the spectacle.

Behind the procession of acrobats and dancers came a trio of male jugglers dressed in white silk tunics with jewelled scarab belts around their waists. Everyone smiled, including the girls, when they saw the men were juggling large, shiny, fake rubies.

'At least, I *guess* they're fake!' Lauren laughed.

The jugglers were followed by magicians, who quickly began to amuse the crowds with their tricks. One of them, a young woman dressed in a pink tunic and an elaborate beaded Egyptian head-dress, came over to the girls.

'Welcome to the court of Queen Cleopatra!'

she said with a smile. 'May I?' She took the parasol from Jas's glass and made it disappear before the girls' very eyes. Then, as they watched, the magician produced it again from behind Jas's ear. The surprised look on Jas's face made Lauren, Mia and Becky howl with laughter.

By the time the girls had finished their fruit drinks, the crowds around the glass cabinets had started to thin out a little. They gave their glasses to a passing waiter and hurried over to take a look at the collection, weaving their way around the tireless performers.

'These are awesome!' Jas gasped, staring at a matching set of gold and ruby earrings, bracelet and necklace. All the gold was fashioned in the shape of sinuous, twisting snakes with ruby eyes. 'I can just imagine Cleopatra, Queen of the Nile, wearing these.'

Lauren and Mia were gazing at a cabinet of diamond and ruby bangles while Becky was mesmerized by a display of ruby rings with large, fiery stones, some set in gold and others matched with diamonds or creamy pearls.

'There aren't any price tags on the jewellery, have you noticed?' Jas murmured as they moved around the collection. 'I wonder if I should ask for one of the pieces for Christmas?'

'Go on then, I dare you!' Lauren retorted with a grin.

The girls had now reached the final display case, the one holding the legendary Cleopatra necklace. The case was made of extra-thick glass, and there were alarms with flashing red lights both inside and outside. The girls clustered around, staring eagerly at the shining golden collar with its glowing teardrop ruby while the security guards looked on impassively.

'That is *so* beautiful,' Mia said softly, gazing into the ruby's fiery depths. 'I wonder if it really *did* belong to Cleopatra.'

'It's going to match Isabella's red dress perfectly,' Becky pointed out. 'I still wish she'd worn the ruby heels, though,' she added wistfully.

'How much is the necklace *really* worth?' Jas asked one of the security men.

'More than you could ever imagine, miss,' he replied gruffly. 'Millions of dollars. It's absolutely priceless.'

Jas turned to the others. 'I don't think I'll be getting *that* for Christmas, then!'

'Does it look anything like the fake necklace Max had in his briefcase?' Becky whispered.

'Exactly the same,' Mia replied. 'I couldn't tell them apart, could you, Jas?'

Jas shook her head.

'Ladies and gentlemen,' announced Antonio Kaspari at that moment, 'I would now like to ask you to accompany me to Ancient Egypt – and meet the Queen of the Nile herself!'

The acrobats immediately somersaulted and back-flipped their way over to the doors. The dancers, musicians and jugglers followed, beckoning the guests to go with them to the next room.

The girls joined the crowd, Becky turning round to catch one final glimpse of the necklace. The security men were now conferring in low voices and one of them was on his walkie-talkie checking with other guards around the gallery as they prepared to open the display case and remove the necklace for Isabella to wear.

As the girls followed the other guests out into the wide passageway, they all exclaimed with delight. Girls in Egyptian robes lined both sides holding woven baskets of red rose petals that they were tossing on the ground in front of the guests as they passed by. At the bottom of the passageway two fire-eaters guarded the doorway into the next room, tipping their heads back and thrusting the burning brands down their throats.

'Wow, look at this room!' Lauren gasped as the four of them went inside. 'It's so – so – *Egyptian*!'

The room had been transformed into an Egyptian palace. The backdrop was a view of marble columns, with the River Nile winding away into the distance. Hieroglyphics adorned the walls, and there were tall, carved wooden statues of Egyptian gods, and exotic palms in painted pots. In the middle of the set was a white silk chaise longue surrounded by open treasure chests with gold and ruby jewellery spilling out of them.

The acrobats and other performers were now standing on the set, frozen in various positions like statues. Suddenly there was a huge explosion of dazzling red smoke in the middle of the room, which made everyone jump. When the smoke cleared, Isabella was standing there, striking a pose, gorgeous in her luscious red dress.

'She must have come up through a trap-door in the floor or something!' Jas guessed, applauding madly along with everyone else. 'Isn't this *spectacular*?'

Music echoed around the room as Isabella was escorted by two of the acrobats to the chaise longue, where she sat down. Her dress seemed to glow under the lights and she wore several bracelets on each wrist and a pair of earrings from the new Kaspari collection. But all eyes, including the girls', were drawn to the ruby and gold necklace that was now around her neck. The ruby glittered fiercely, sending darts of twinkling light all over the room.

'Oh, I'm so glad Isabella invited us!' Mia said breathlessly, taking out her camera.

The whole set now burst into life as the acrobats began to tumble again, the jugglers to juggle, and the dancers formed a half-circle around Isabella, swaying in time to the music. The photographers were allowed to come forward now to take their pictures of Isabella while the security guards watched from the back of the room, walkie-talkies in hand, their eyes constantly scanning the crowd. The acrobats cartwheeled and somersaulted their way around the set, carefully selecting pieces that were part of the new collection from the treasure chests and then offering them to Isabella to try on.

Becky watched as the actress was photographed in a variety of poses wearing different pieces from the collection. It was a spectacular show. And even though Isabella's behaviour had been a bit unpredictable and diva-ish, it had been worth it, Becky thought. She wouldn't have missed this for the world.

All too soon, the photo-shoot was over. Smiling, Isabella waved at the applauding crowd. Then, as the security men moved towards her, she reached behind her and undid the clasp of the necklace.

'Let me help you, Miss Duval,' said one of the guards, hurrying forward.

'Don't worry,' Isabella began, 'I've done it – oh!' She lost her grip on the necklace and it slithered down the front of her red gown out of sight. Everyone laughed and applauded as, looking a little pink and embarrassed, Isabella fished it out and handed it to the guard. Quickly the two men hurried off to replace the necklace in its display case.

'Isabella, it's time for us to leave.' Max had rushed across the room to the actress's side. 'You must rest, you know. We have a flight to catch this afternoon.'

'I thought Isabella was going to stay and chat to the guests,' Becky whispered to Mia, Jas and Lauren, looking very disappointed. 'That's what she told us in the spa, anyway.'

'She must have changed her mind,' Jas sighed.

'Maybe she's not feeling too well. Let's go and watch her leave, shall we?'

Isabella was saying her goodbyes to Antonio Kaspari and the organizers of the launch. Mr Kaspari and the others were clearly somewhat bemused by this sudden departure and it seemed they were trying to persuade her to change her mind. But Isabella was pouting crossly and shaking her head.

'Isabella's having another diva moment!' Lauren whispered to Becky.

Becky nodded. She could see that Max was urging Isabella along, clearly reluctant to stay at the event a moment longer. As the girls watched Isabella and Max hurry out of the gallery to the top of the steps, Becky suddenly had an uneasy feeling, as if something was very, very wrong. At first she didn't know what. Then, as she gazed at Max and Isabella standing side by side, she realized *exactly* what was bothering her.

'Isabella is the same height as Max!' Becky burst out.

Jas, Mia and Lauren turned to stare at her in surprise.

'Don't you remember when Isabella tried on the ruby heels in her hotel suite?' Becky went on. 'She was the same height as Max – but *only when she was wearing the killer heels*. Now she's wearing flats, so how can she be the same height as him?'

'You're obsessed with shoes, Becky!' Jas began with a grin, but Lauren shook her head.

'Let's think this through a minute,' she said slowly, glancing at Max and Isabella as they went down the red carpet. There were still some die-hard fans hanging around outside, and they began pestering Isabella again for autographs and photos, slowing her progress. 'Becky's right. It *is* odd.'

'It's not just odd – it's *impossible*,' Mia chimed in. 'Unless Max has shrunk!'

'He can't have!' Becky said, puzzled. 'And *he* wasn't wearing heels that day, was he?'

'No, only Isabella was,' Jas replied.

'So how can he and Isabella now be the same height?' Lauren wondered.

The girls stared at each other in bewilderment.

'This just can't be right!' Becky shook her head. 'Either Isabella has grown taller or Max has got shorter, and both of those things are impossible—'

'OH!' Jas burst out suddenly, her face lighting up with intense excitement. 'There is one explanation – and it's the only one I can think of.

What if Isabella is actually someone else? Someone taller?'

Becky, Mia and Lauren looked confused.

'Jas, are you sure you didn't have a sip of that pink champagne?' Lauren asked teasingly.

But Jas was shaking her head fiercely. 'No, I mean, seriously – what if there are TWO Isabellas?'

CHAPTER NINE

Becky, Mia and Lauren looked completely stunned at Jas's outburst.

'I know, I know, it's ridiculous,' Jas gabbled, hardly able to believe it herself, even though she was the one who'd said it. 'But if you think about it, it's the only thing that makes sense.'

'Two Isabellas *would* explain everything,' Becky said slowly. 'One's short and one's tall.'

'One loves ice-cream and one hates it,' Lauren added.

'And one's nice and friendly while the other's a super-diva!' Mia exclaimed. 'You're brilliant, Jas!'

'Thank you,' Jas said modestly. 'So we're agreed then, however crazy it sounds, that there might be two Isabellas? And the one who came to the exhibition is the fake, and that's why she's the same height as Max even without heels?' She glanced down the steps at Isabella, who was still signing autographs for the fans.

'But why are there *two* Isabellas?' Lauren asked with a frown.

'Not just two Isabellas,' Mia pointed out. 'Two Isabellas and *two* ruby necklaces as well. Lauren's right, it doesn't make any sense.'

But suddenly the answer popped straight into Lauren's head from nowhere. 'It *does* make sense – *if* Max and the fake Isabella have stolen the real ruby necklace and put the replica in its place!' she declared triumphantly. 'Two Isabellas and two ruby necklaces! See?'

Becky, Mia and Jas stared at her, open-mouthed.

'The necklace was only loaned to Kaspari by that American museum so that Isabella could wear it at the launch,' Lauren explained breath-lessly. 'If the real Isabella wasn't in on the plot, then Max would have needed a fake Isabella to take her place and make the switch. Then Max and Fake Isabella zoom off somewhere on a plane, taking the priceless necklace with them!'

'I think you're right, Lauren!' Becky slapped her friend admiringly on the back. '*That's* why Max had a copy of the necklace in his briefcase. He and Fake Isabella needed it to make the swap so that no one would suspect them and they could make their getaway.'

'But when could they have done it?' Mia began, and then she gave a yelp of excitement. 'Oh, I think I know! When Isabella dropped the necklace down the front of her dress during the photo-shoot, everyone thought it was an accident, but maybe it *wasn't*. She could have had the fake necklace hidden there already, waiting to swap it with the real one.'

'Yes, the only time the necklace was out of its display case was when Fake Isabella was wearing it,' Becky pointed out.

'So we were right about Max all along.' Jas shot him a disgusted look. He was now trying to coax Isabella away from her fans and into the red limo. 'He might not have taken Mrs Lloyd's watch, but he's still a crook!'

Now that the first excitement was over, though, Lauren was beginning to feel a little nervous.

'OK, so now we *think* we've stumbled onto a plot to steal the ruby necklace,' she said hesitantly, 'and so far Max and Fake Isabella think they've got away with it. But, guys, we have to be sure before we say anything to anyone. This is huge!'

'Lauren's right.' Becky bit her lip. 'This is heaps bigger than Max stealing an antique watch.'

'And we were wrong *then*,' Mia reminded everyone. 'We've got to be absolutely certain we're right this time. It would be really unfair if we accused Max without any proof.'

'Yes, and who's going to believe there are two Isabella Duvals unless we can prove it somehow?' Jas agreed.

'And where's the *real* Isabella, anyway?' Becky asked, looking worried. 'Do you think she's still at the hotel? I hope she's OK.'

'We'd better go and check,' Mia said. 'Max would have had to stop her from coming to the launch somehow, for his plan to work.'

They heard the sound of a car door slam and saw the fake Isabella settling down in the back seat of the limo. Max had shut the door and was walking round to the other side of the car to get inside himself. If they were right, Jas speculated, then the *real* necklace was still hidden down the front of the fake Isabella's dress. And the replica necklace had been put in the display cabinet by the security guards. So . . .

'I've got it!' Jas gasped. 'We need to go back to the hotel to check on Isabella, so we can also look to see if the fake necklace is still in Max's briefcase. If it is, then we know it hasn't been switched for the real one, and he's in the clear.'

'Then we'd also know we've got it all wrong about Max,' Becky agreed, 'and that there must be some other explanation for the change in Isabella's height.'

'We've got to get back to the hotel before Max and Isabella, though,' Mia said. 'And look, they're already on their way . . .'

The chauffeur had started up the limo but he was only able to move forward very slowly because there were still fans and photographers surrounding the car. The police were helping to move them aside.

Lauren turned to the others. 'It's going to take them a while to get back to the hotel,' she declared, her eyes alight with excitement. 'You know how bad the traffic was when my mum dropped us off. Well, we can beat them there if we make a run for it!'

'Let's go right away!' And Jas headed for the steps. She was determined to stop Max and the fake Isabella from getting away with the necklace, if they could. What a nerve they had to think they could steal it from under the nose of everyone, including Mr Kaspari himself!

'Wait!' Lauren shrieked. She kicked off her high heels and opened the evening bag her mum had lent her. She took out a pair of flats and slipped them on, scooping up her wedge heels and cramming them into the bag when she'd done so. The others stared at her in amazement.

'Well, I knew my feet would be killing me after an hour or two, so I shoved my flatties in the bag to change into,' Lauren confessed. 'And now I'm glad I did because I would have broken my neck running in heels! Come on, you lot. There's no time to lose!'

The four girls ran down the red carpet and pushed their way through the throng of fans still hanging around the limo. Then they dashed off down the street.

'How are we going to get into Max's room?' Jas panted, swerving around a passer-by.

'We'll need a skeleton key-card.' Lauren was battling to find her phone in her handbag as she ran. 'You know, the ones that open every door in the hotel. We won't have time to get one ourselves, but I've got an idea . . .' She hit speed dial, side-stepping a young mum with a pushchair. Jas wondered who on earth Lauren was calling.

'Hello, Charlie?' Lauren gasped. 'I've got a mission for you. No, just be quiet and listen to me – a secret agent doesn't ask questions! I want you to go and borrow a skeleton key-card for me from behind the hotel reception desk. Don't let anyone see you, OK? And when you've got it, go to the front doors of the hotel and wait for us there. No, I'll explain later – just do it! 'Bye.'

'This is really risky, Lauren,' Becky puffed. 'What if Charlie gets caught? You'll be in megatrouble with your parents.'

'I know,' Lauren said solemnly. 'But we haven't got time to come up with another plan – not with Max and the other Isabella on their way back to the hotel!'

Jas felt even more nervous as they hurtled round the corner and down the road that led to the hotel. There were so many things that could go wrong with the plan. As Becky had said, Charlie might get spotted taking the key-card, but not only that: they might get caught in Max's room searching his briefcase. Even with the busy traffic, Max and the fake Isabella could only be a few minutes behind them. Or The Snoop might be lurking around the corridors . . . *And what if we've jumped to all the wrong conclusions and there's some innocent explanation for everything?* Jas thought uneasily. It wasn't only Lauren who'd be in big trouble with her parents then. It would be all of them.

Everything depended on whether the replica necklace was still inside Max's briefcase or not . . .

CHAPTER TEN

'Look, there are more TV crews, photographers and fans waiting for Isabella outside the Mayfair Park,' Becky pointed out as the girls neared the hotel.

'That's good,' Lauren said. 'It might slow Isabella and Max down a bit and give us more time.' As they hurried up the steps, she peered anxiously into reception, looking for Charlie. Would her brother have managed to get the skeleton key-card or not? If he hadn't, Lauren would have to try and get hold of one herself, and that would lose them precious minutes.

As James swung the glass door open for them with a smile, Lauren felt a huge wave of relief wash over her. She'd spotted Charlie and Joe waiting for them, lurking behind one of the tall potted plants in the foyer.

'Did you get the key-card?' Lauren asked, rushing over to the boys.

'Ssh!' Charlie said indignantly. 'The enemy might hear!' And very carefully he slid the key-card into Lauren's hand, keeping it out of sight of everyone passing by. 'Dad's gone out to a business meeting so I sneaked into his office and borrowed his.'

'Charlie, I could kiss you!' Jas declared, beaming at him. 'And you too, Joe!'

The boys looked horrified.

'No, thanks,' Joe said quickly.

'What's going on, anyway?' Charlie asked.

'We haven't got time to tell you the whole story now,' Lauren said, 'but it all started when we noticed that Isabella had grown taller since we first met her!'

Charlie and Joe stared at each other in bemusement.

'What's so strange about that?' Charlie said. 'I sometimes grow a couple of centimetres a week!'

'Just cover for us, will you, and try to make sure Mum and Dad don't notice the missing key-card,' Lauren told him. 'It's *really* important—'

'Charlie!'

Lauren glanced at the other girls in dismay as her mum hurried across reception towards them. Quickly she slipped the key-card into her pocket.

'Hello, girls.' Mrs Bond smiled at them. 'Did you enjoy the launch?'

'It was fantastic, Mum,' Lauren said quickly, wondering how they could get away without seeming too impatient. 'We're just going upstairs.'

'To get changed?' her mum asked, but luckily she didn't wait for a reply. Instead she turned to Charlie and gave him a stern look. 'Didn't I ask you to tidy your bedroom this morning, young man?'

'Um – I forgot,' Charlie muttered sheepishly. 'Anyway, Lauren's is worse than mine!'

'Lauren's next on my list!' Mrs Bond said. 'But *after* the other girls have got changed and gone home. Am I going to have to stand over you to make you do it, Charles Bond? I will if I have to!'

Charlie opened his mouth to protest, but then he glanced at Lauren as if a thought had just struck him. 'OK,' he muttered, 'that's probably a good idea.'

'Right then,' Mrs Bond agreed briskly. 'Go upstairs and make a start and I'll be there in five minutes to keep an eye on you.' And she hurried off.

'That'll keep Mum out of your way for the next hour or so!' Charlie whispered to Lauren.

'Charlie, you're a star!' Jas said.

As the girls rushed off towards the lift, they heard Joe say, 'I don't have to help clean your bedroom, do I, Charlie?'

'Course you do,' Charlie replied firmly. 'This is a secret agent mission, so stop moaning!'

The girls waited impatiently in the lift as it rose up towards the ninth floor. Lauren could hardly stand still and her heart was beating so hard it was thundering in her ears. If her parents ever found out she was about to use a key-card to enter a guest's room, she'd be in SO much trouble, she *totally* didn't want to think about it . . .

When the lift doors opened, Lauren and the others didn't dare run along the corridor to Max's room in case The Snoop was lurking. So they power-walked as fast as they could without actually running.

'Here goes,' Lauren murmured, inserting the key-card into the slot. The green light flashed and she opened the door.

The room was neat and tidy, with nothing out of place except for Max's briefcase, which lay on the bed. Jas was first to reach it and, her face full of anticipation, she fumbled with the catches.

'It's locked!' she groaned, burying her head

in her hands. 'I don't *believe* it. What now?'

'Actually,' Mia put in, 'I saw Max unlock it when we were hiding under the bed. And I *think* I remember the code. Try four-eight-three-two, Jas.'

Jas punched in the numbers and gave a shriek of triumph as the catches clicked and the brief-case opened.

'Ssh!' Lauren warned her. 'The Snoop might be passing by!'

'Sorry,' Jas whispered, flinging the lid of the briefcase open. 'Thank goodness you've got a good head for numbers, Mia.'

'Is the fake necklace in there?' Becky asked, peering over Jas's shoulder.

The briefcase was half full of papers and documents, but there was no sign of the necklace.

'It looks like you were right, Jas,' Lauren declared. 'Max and the fake Isabella *have* stolen the real necklace. So the one now on display in the cabinet at the gallery must be the fake!'

'We have to stop them getting away with it,' Becky said urgently. 'But I'm *really* worried about Isabella too. What do you think they've done with her?'

'Let's go up to her suite and check,' Mia suggested.

The girls made their way back to the lifts as quickly as they could and headed for the Ruby Suite on the top floor.

'Look, there's a *Do Not Disturb* sign hanging on Isabella's door,' Jas pointed out when they reached the suite.

Lauren hesitated. 'No one's supposed to go into a guest's room when that sign's outside,' she said.

'But this *is* an emergency!' Becky pointed out. Lauren nodded. She slotted the key-card into the lock and swung open the door.

The Ruby Suite was dark and quiet, and all the curtains were drawn. The girls tiptoed inside, but there was no sign of Isabella in the living-room. Jas peeped into the bathroom while Becky went over to the bedroom.

'Girls!' Becky called suddenly. 'Over here!'

Lauren, Jas and Mia rushed to the bedroom. The curtains around the four-poster bed were drawn, but Becky had pulled one of them aside. The other girls were stunned to see Isabella lying slumped on the bed, fast asleep and breathing heavily. She was wearing the red dress and the ruby high-heeled shoes – her outfit for the launch.

'Do you think she's OK?' Becky asked nervously.

As the girls stared at Isabella in confusion, the actress began to stir. It took her a moment or two to open her eyes and then she blinked drowsily, gazing up at them as if she wasn't quite sure who they were.

'Wh-what's going on?' Isabella asked, her voice croaky and dry. She tried to sit up but seemed dazed and disorientated. Becky and Jas rushed to help her. 'What time is it?'

'I'll get a glass of water,' Mia said, and ran out.

Isabella was now blinking down at her watch. 'Oh no,' she gasped, 'I should have been at the jewellery launch hours ago – and now I've missed it!' She put her hand to her head, looking bleary-eyed and upset. 'What happened to me? I feel terrible.'

'What's the last thing you remember, Isabella?' Becky asked gently.

Isabella frowned. 'I don't know,' she sighed as Mia handed her a glass of water. 'My mind seems to be a complete blank.' She took a sip and then glanced at the girls in shock. 'Oh, *now* I remember! Max gave me a glass of water and I drank it and then – well, I must have fallen asleep.'

Lauren glanced at Mia, Jas and Becky. 'I think Isabella was drugged so she'd sleep through the whole of the launch,' she said. 'That would give Max and the other Isabella the perfect opportunity to swap the replica necklace for the real one.'

'Max must have had the exact same red dress made for the fake Isabella,' Becky added, gazing at Isabella's gown. 'This one would have been much too short for her and it would have given the game away.'

'And maybe it had a secret pocket sewn into it to hide the stolen necklace in,' Jas suggested eagerly.

Isabella stared at Lauren, Becky and Jas in amazement. 'Max . . . fake Isabella . . . stolen necklace,' she repeated. 'What *are* you talking about?'

'I think I'd better make Isabella an extra-strong cup of coffee,' Mia said, heading out of the room again. 'She's going to need it!'

Ten minutes and one very strong cup of coffee later, Isabella was now fully awake and alert, although she had a splitting headache. She sat and listened intently as the girls explained everything that had happened, looking as if she could hardly believe it.

'How could Max *do* such a thing?' Isabella kept saying. 'I thought we were *friends*. He must have been planning this for ages.' She was obviously upset and confused. Lauren felt very sorry for her, and she could see that the others did too.

'The question is, what happens now?' Jas asked.

'I suppose we'd better call the police,' Lauren said. Although it seemed the girls had been right all along, she still wasn't looking forward to explaining everything to her mum and dad.

'Ssh!' Mia put her finger to her lips. 'I can hear voices.'

'Someone's outside the door,' Becky whispered, 'and it sounds like Max and the fake Isabella!'

CHAPTER ELEVEN

The girls and Isabella stared at each other in horror.

'Pretend you're still asleep, Isabella,' Becky hissed, 'and we'll hide somewhere until they've gone.'

Looking a little frightened, Isabella lay down and closed her eyes while Becky drew the curtain around the bed again. Then Jas led the girls into the bathroom and shut the door quietly behind them. Just a few seconds later they heard the sound of a key-card being inserted into the lock. Jas pressed her ear to the door, her heart thumping so hard she could hardly breathe.

The girls heard footsteps hurrying into the suite.

'Looks like everything is OK here,' Max said with satisfaction. 'I'll just check on Isabella and make sure she's still asleep.'

'Hurry up, then,' the fake Isabella called petulantly. 'I was really nervous with all those police and security guards around at the launch. Now we've got the necklace, I want to get out of here right away.'

'Just calm down, Suzanne!' Max snapped as the girls heard him open the door to the bedroom and go in. 'Everything's going to be OK.'

Jas glanced at Becky, Mia and Lauren and silently mouthed *Suzanne!* at them. The fake Isabella was the woman she and Mia had heard in Max's room when they'd been hiding under the bed! Jas just prayed that neither Max nor Suzanne wanted to use the bathroom for any reason . . .

'That's easy for *you* to say,' Suzanne complained bitterly. '*I'm* the one who had to do all the hard work impersonating Isabella and stealing the necklace. I'm scared something's going to go wrong right at the last minute.'

'Look, no one suspects a thing,' Max went on confidently as he came out of the bedroom again. 'Isabella's still asleep, and the plan worked beautifully. I don't want to hang around any more than you do. We've got a plane to catch and a buyer for the necklace waiting for us in South America. Let's go.'

Jas and the others waited until they heard the door of the Ruby Suite close behind the two thieves. Then they rushed out of the bathroom. Isabella was struggling unsteadily to her feet, her face pale and angry.

'Girls, we *have* to stop those crooks from getting away with this!' she said.

'You ring the police, Isabella,' Jas told her. 'We'll go down and try to stall Max and the fake Isabella until they get here.'

Isabella nodded. Lauren threw open the door of the Ruby Suite and this time the girls tore along the corridor to the lifts at top speed.

'If we bump into The Snoop, it's just too bad,' Becky declared, pushing the button to call the lift. 'This is *definitely* an emergency!'

The lift seemed to take ages to arrive, and then another hundred years to move down between the floors. Jas could have screamed with impatience. She imagined Max and Suzanne jumping into their limo, whizzing off to the airport and flying out of the country before anyone could stop them. She glanced up at the display above the lift doors and saw that they were only at the third floor.

'Come on, come on!' Jas muttered to herself.

'How on earth are we going to stall Max and Suzanne?' Mia asked as the lift finally came to a stop.

'I don't know – but we'll think of something!' Lauren replied.

The lift doors opened and the girls rushed out. To Jas's intense relief, Max and Suzanne were only just leaving the hotel. Max was carrying his briefcase and Suzanne was still dressed in the ruby gown that exactly matched Isabella's. The minute they stepped outside, there was a frenzy of camera flashes as the paparazzi began snapping photos.

Jas, Mia, Becky and Lauren dashed after them. They saw Max whisper something to Suzanne, and she began smiling for the TV cameras and the photographers and waving at the cheering fans, but Jas could see that she was anxious to get away.

'They're leaving!' Lauren whispered when, after a few moments, Max began to hurry Suzanne down the steps towards the waiting car.

Jas racked her brains desperately for some way to stop the pair of thieves making their getaway. There was only one thing she could think of . . .

'STOP THAT WOMAN!' Jas yelled at the top of her voice, pointing at Suzanne. 'She's not Isabella Duval at all. SHE'S A FAKE!'

In the space of just a few seconds, the whole of the crowd fell silent and the photographers stopped taking pictures. Everyone turned to look at Jas, including Max and Suzanne, who both shot poisonous glares at her. Jas gulped. *I've really gone and done it now*, she thought.

'Well, you've certainly managed to stall them, Jas!' Lauren whispered in her ear.

'What are you talking about?' Suzanne demanded, quickly regaining her poise. As the crowd began to mutter curiously amongst themselves, she tossed her head angrily and turned to Max. 'Get me out of here right now, please,' Suzanne said in an outraged voice. 'I don't want to hear this ridiculous nonsense.'

'Sorry, folks, Isabella has a plane to catch,' Max called apologetically. But he and Suzanne couldn't get through as journalists and TV reporters instantly crowded around them.

'Would you like to comment on this "fake Isabella" allegation?' one of the TV reporters asked, sticking a microphone under Max's nose.

Suddenly the sound of a police siren filled the

air and a moment later a police car drew up next to Max and Suzanne's limo.

'They got here quickly,' Mia said with relief.

Two uniformed policemen climbed out of their car, and Jas, Becky, Mia and Lauren hurried down the steps towards them.

'Do you require some assistance, Miss Duval?' one of the policemen asked Suzanne.

'No, she doesn't – but we do!' Jas butted in breathlessly. 'And *she's* not Isabella Duval. She's a fake!'

'They've stolen the antique ruby necklace from the Columbine Gallery!' Lauren announced, pointing at Max and Suzanne. She saw Suzanne turn pale and clutch Max's arm as the two policemen glanced at each other.

'Well, *we've* just come from the gallery,' the second policeman said, staring at Lauren suspiciously. 'We were there to help out with security and crowd control for the launch. And for your information' – he raised his eyebrows – 'the ruby necklace was safely locked away in its display case when we left.'

'It's a fake,' Mia explained. 'Suzanne – the other Isabella – switched the necklaces when she was doing the photo-shoot.'

'You have to arrest them before they leave the

country!' Jas added, glaring at Max and Suzanne.

The watching crowd began murmuring to each other in amazement. But Max just shrugged and shook his head.

'This is utterly ridiculous,' he said smoothly, smiling at the policemen. 'If you should arrest *anyone*, Officer, it's these silly girls. They've been pestering Isabella ever since she arrived at the hotel.'

Becky could see that the policemen seemed to believe what Max was saying. Swallowing down her frustration, she put on her most grown-up voice.

'Look, there's a really simple way to see if we're telling the truth or not,' Becky said. 'Just check their bags and see if the necklace is in there.' And she pointed at Max's briefcase and Suzanne's patent leather designer tote. 'Doesn't it seem a bit strange that they're travelling so light? It's obviously because they're in such a hurry to leave the country.'

Everyone in the crowd now stared at Max and Suzanne's bags.

'Nonsense!' Max retorted. 'Our luggage is being sent on after us, that's all. Look, officers, these girls' – he threw a furious glance at Becky, Mia, Jas and Lauren – 'have been nothing but trouble since we arrived. They've been hounding Isabella and upsetting her.'

Suzanne was nodding in agreement. 'Most of my fans are lovely,' she said in a tearful voice. 'But *sometimes* there are one or two who just won't leave me alone, and they make my life very difficult . . .'

The girls glanced at each other in horror as the crowd began to make sympathetic noises.

'I think we've heard enough,' the first policeman said, gazing sternly at Jas, Mia, Becky and Lauren. 'Stand back now, girls.'

'Thank you, officers,' Max said gratefully. 'I'd be extremely obliged if we could leave immediately. We do have a plane to catch.'

'Certainly, sir,' the policeman agreed.

'It looks like Max and Suzanne are going to get away with it!' Becky whispered furiously as the policemen began to move them aside so that Suzanne and Max could pass. 'What shall we do?'

But suddenly a stunned hush fell over the crowd. Becky, Mia, Jas and Lauren saw that everyone was now staring up at the hotel behind Max and Suzanne. The girls turned round too, and Becky's heart began to pound with excitement.

The *real* Isabella, dressed in the flowing red gown and high-heeled ruby shoes, was standing at the top of the steps.

CHAPTER TWELVE

For a moment there was an amazed silence as everyone stared back and forth from the fake to the real Isabella, both wearing identical red gowns. No one seemed to know what to do or what to say, including the two policemen. Becky glanced at Suzanne and Max. Both of them now looked white-faced and apprehensive.

Then Suzanne pointed angrily at Isabella. '*She's* the fake!' she shrieked. 'Not me!'

Suddenly it seemed to Becky that everyone was talking at once. The reporters were all pushing forward and shouting questions while the crowd of fans were asking each other what on earth was going on. Meanwhile the police were trying to calm the situation while looking as bewildered as everyone else. In the midst of the din, Suzanne tried to push her way through to the car, but one of the policemen stopped her.

Everyone's gaze turned to Isabella again, but

she didn't say anything. Instead, she simply bent over and slipped off her ruby shoes. Then she straightened up and smiled at the crowd.

'I think you know I'm famous for being quite short!' Isabella announced, her eyes twinkling. 'Surely you can all see now that this is the real me?'

There were shouts of agreement from some of Isabella's fans, and Mia, Becky, Jas and Lauren smiled at each other with utter relief.

'I think somebody has some explaining to do,' one of the policemen said, a steely look in his eyes as he and his colleague moved closer to Max and Suzanne.

'Officers, I know who this woman is.' Amidst a flurry of camera flashes, Isabella put her shoes back on, picked up her long skirt and walked down the steps to applause from her loyal fans, including the girls. 'She's Suzanne Armitage. She makes a living as an Isabella Duval lookalike, and she was my body double in my last film. And this, of course' – Isabella shot Max a look of disgust – 'is my *former* assistant, Max Carroll.'

Max and Suzanne both glared at Isabella. Then Suzanne looked shocked as one of the policemen held out his hand.

'May we have a look inside your bag, Miss Armitage?' he asked.

'This is outrageous!' Suzanne spluttered. 'It's an invasion of my privacy!'

'This is all a terrible mistake,' Max added. But Becky could see by his face that he knew the game was up.

Suzanne had no choice but to give the policeman her bag. Becky, Mia, Jas and Lauren watched impatiently as the policeman searched through it. Suddenly he gave an exclamation and slowly drew out the gold necklace. There was a moment of stunned silence as he held it aloft and everyone stared at the teardrop ruby glittering in the sunlight. Then there were gasps and rousing cheers from the crowd, and a storm of flashguns popped as the photographers jostled to get the best shots.

'Guys, we did it!' Jas proclaimed happily, watching as the two policemen put a grim-faced Max and Suzanne under arrest.

'It was close though, wasn't it?' Becky sighed.

Mia nodded. 'I really thought Max and Suzanne were going to talk themselves out of it!'

'Girls, you were wonderful!' Isabella declared, giving each of them a huge hug. 'I'm *so* grateful.'

'Can we have an interview, girls?' one of the

TV reporters called, waving her microphone.

'How did you know that Max and Suzanne were the thieves?' a journalist shouted.

'Can you tell us exactly how they swapped the two necklaces?' another hollered as Max and Suzanne were escorted to the police car.

'I think you four girls are going to be just as famous as I am!' Isabella laughed. 'This will be all over the TV and the newspapers.'

'Wow!' Jas gasped.

'Awesome!' Lauren agreed. Then she spotted a car that had just pulled up outside the hotel. Mr Bond, returning from his business meeting, was looking bemused as he climbed out of his car and took in the police, the noisy crowd, Isabella Duval and Lauren, Becky, Jas and Mia in the middle of it all. Meanwhile, Mrs Bond had appeared at the top of the steps, flanked by Charlie and Joe, and she too looked totally bewildered.

'Before we give any interviews . . .' Lauren said with a grin, 'I've got to work out exactly how I'm going to explain all this to my parents!'

'You're still alive then, Lauren!' Jas said, smiling, as the girls took the lift up to the Ruby Suite early the following morning. Isabella was preparing to leave the hotel and fly back to the States, and she'd asked the girls to pop in and see her briefly to say goodbye before they went to school.

'Yes, just.' Lauren pulled a comical face. 'Mum and Dad were pretty good about it, considering. They were a bit annoyed with me for not telling them we were suspicious of Max, but I explained that we didn't have any proof.'

'Is Charlie OK about missing out on most of the excitement outside the hotel?' Becky asked with a grin.

Lauren nodded. 'He's more annoyed about the fact that he and Joe didn't notice there was anything suspicious about Max until we told him so. The last thing I heard, he and Joe were searching online for ways to spot if someone's a criminal or not!'

The girls laughed.

'At least we've got *loads* of material for our Media Studies project now,' Mia remarked as they got out of the lift. 'My mum and dad went out and bought all the newspapers this morning!'

As Isabella had predicted, the sensational story of the attempted theft of the ruby necklace was all over the media. Pictures of the girls and Isabella, as well as Max and Suzanne, were splashed across the front pages, and all the news channels had made it their headline story.

'I know,' Becky laughed. 'Even my dad was thrilled that we'd got the necklace back, and I don't think he knows who Isabella is!'

'It's *totally* embarrassing seeing yourself on TV though, isn't it?' Jas added as she rang the bell of the Ruby Suite. 'And my family recorded all the news programmes and insisted on playing them over and over again last night!'

At that moment the door opened.

'Hi, girls,' Isabella cried with a smile. 'Come in. I'm almost ready to leave.'

The girls went into the suite. Isabella's bags and suitcases lay around the room, and there were four sparkly silver boxes piled up on the coffee-table.

'I know I said all my thank-yous yesterday,' Isabella went on earnestly, 'but I just wanted to make sure you knew how grateful I was. Kaspari are very pleased that the necklace has been returned too.'

'We were glad to help,' Becky said, beaming at her.

'These are just little gifts from me to say thank you again.' Isabella went over to the table and started handing out the silver boxes. 'This one's for you, Becky. And this is for Lauren. Jas and Mia, the bottom two boxes have your names on them.'

Becky was first to open her box, pulling aside layers of cream tissue paper. She took out a pair of red, strappy, low-heeled sandals decorated with tiny crystals, and gave a cry of delight.

'Oh, they're by that famous designer, Christian Lee!' Becky breathed, hardly able to believe her eyes. Lauren, Jas and Mia were also squealing with excitement as they unwrapped their own new shoes. They were all red, like Becky's. Mia had a pair of crimson suede kitten heels, while Jas's were round-toed, wedge-heeled scarlet Mary-Janes.

'Yes, Christian's one of my favourite designers as well as a friend of mine,' Isabella explained. 'I rang him yesterday and told him what I wanted and they were delivered last night. Lauren's mum kindly told me your sizes.'

'Thank you!' Jas gasped, kicking off her trainers and slipping her new shoes on immediately. Becky and Mia did the same.

'I got flatties for you, Lauren,' Isabella said as Lauren pulled out a stunning pair of red ballet flats with black satin bows. 'I noticed you don't wear heels.'

'Fantastic!' Lauren gasped.

'I feel like a star myself now,' Mia remarked, parading up and down in her kitten heels.

'We'll think of you every time we wear them, Isabella,' Becky said, giving the star a hug.

'Yes, we'll *never* forget the mysterious Case of the Ruby Necklace!' Jas added with a grin.

If there's a mystery to solve . . . ask the girls from Mayfair Park

Look out for:

THE CASE of the **Poisoned Pie**

And coming Summer 2011

THE CASE of the **Suspicious Supermodel**

THE CASE of the **Haunted House**

bindi babes

by Narinder Dhami

Meet the coolest chicks on the block . . .

These girls have been through tough times,
but now that they've got their perfect world sorted,
the one fashion accessory they don't need is an
interfering live-in auntie trying to cramp their style.

Bring on the collective power of the Bindi Babes!
Nothing in life, not even their formidable auntie-ji,
can stop these sisters . . . can it?

'A fresh voice and fun characters that girls will love'
Jacqueline Wilson

978 0 440 86512 4

THE LADY GRACE MYSTERIES

ASSASSIN

By Grace Cavendish

MURDER AT COURT!

One suitor dead with a knife in his back, and another
under suspicion ... Can Lady Grace, Queen Elizabeth's
favourite Maid of Honour, solve the mystery and
bring order back to the Queen's Court?

Open up the daybook of Lady Grace for a
tale of daggers, death and a very daring girl ...

'A gripping historical thriller' *Sunday Times*

978 1 862 30376 8

witch baby and me
by Debi Gliori

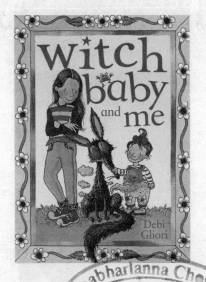

My life is in ruins.
Here's why:
- I have a baby sister called Daisy. She's not a *baby* baby,
  she's a *witch* baby.
- Only *I* know this (that she's a witch baby). Everyone else
  thinks she's sweet and adorable.
- Daisy's summoned up an invisible dog called WayWoof
  to be her pet. People can smell WayWoof but they can't
  see him – so they think the smell is me.

But worst of all is:
- Mum and Dad have decided that we're moving house.
  To the far, far North of Scotland. Which means I'll never
  see my friends again!

**'I can't recommend this story highly enough for lovers of magic,
humour or even books. A wicked triumph'** *Eoin Colfer*

978 0 552 55676 7